W9-DCU-049

LITTLE GREEN MEN VOLUME 3: Small Package, Big Fun!
Copyright © 2011 Ape Entertainment L.L.C. This book constitutes a work of fiction; any resemblance between anyone living or dead and the events and characters in this book is purely coincidental. All rights reserved; with the exception of brief passages for review purposes, no part of this work may be copied, reproduced, or digitally transmitted without the prior written permission from the publisher.
Published by Ape Entertainment, San Diego, CA (www.ApeComics.com). Proudly printed in the USA.

Little GREEN Men

created by
BRENT ERWIN & DAVID HEDGECOCK

SMALL PACKAGE, BIG FUN!

Story, pencil, inks, colors, letters by
JAY FOSGITT

APE ENTERTAINMENT

David Hedgecock
CEO | Partner

Brent E. Erwin
COO | Partner

Kevin Freeman
Editor

Matt Anderson
Editor

Aaron Sparrow
Editor

Rick Lebo
Graphic Design

Company Information:
Ape Entertainment
P.O. Box 7100
San Diego, CA 92167
www.ApeComics.com

For Licensing / Media rights conta
Scott L. Agostoni
email: ScottAgostoni@gmail.com

APE WEBSITE:
ApeComics.com

Special thanks to H.J. Harrison who helps make it all possible.

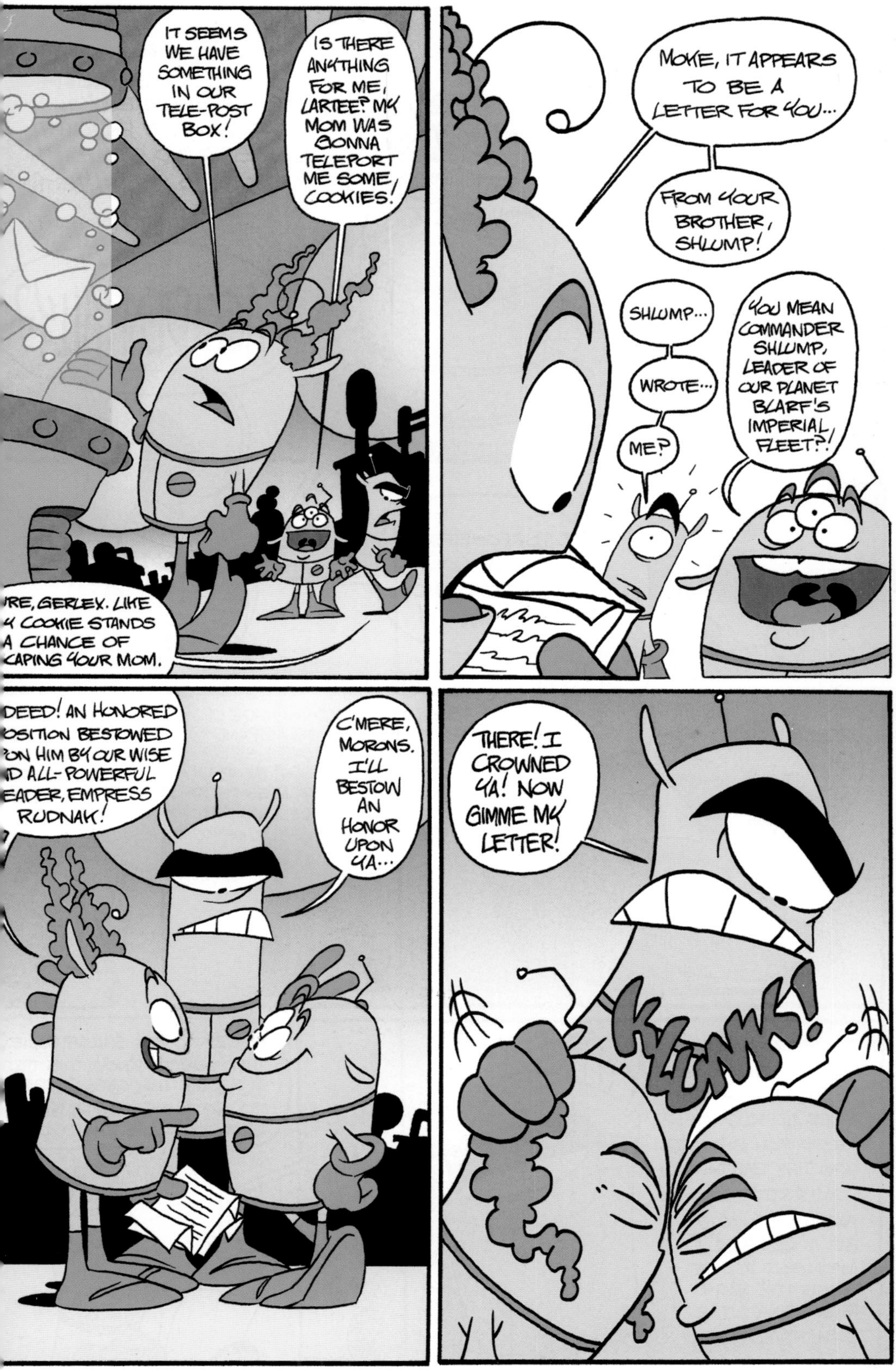
IT SEEMS WE HAVE SOMETHING IN OUR TELE-POST BOX!
IS THERE ANYTHING FOR ME, LARTEE? MY MOM WAS GONNA TELEPORT ME SOME COOKIES!
RE, GERLEX. LIKE COOKIE STANDS A CHANCE OF CAPING YOUR MOM.
MOKE, IT APPEARS TO BE A LETTER FOR YOU...
FROM YOUR BROTHER, SHLUMP!
SHLUMP...
WROTE...
ME?
YOU MEAN COMMANDER SHLUMP, LEADER OF OUR PLANET BLARF'S IMPERIAL FLEET?!
DEED! AN HONORED OSITION BESTOWED ON HIM BY OUR WISE D ALL-POWERFUL EADER, EMPRESS RUDNAK!
C'MERE, MORONS. I'LL BESTOW AN HONOR UPON YA...
THERE! I CROWNED YA! NOW GIMME MY LETTER!
KLUNK!

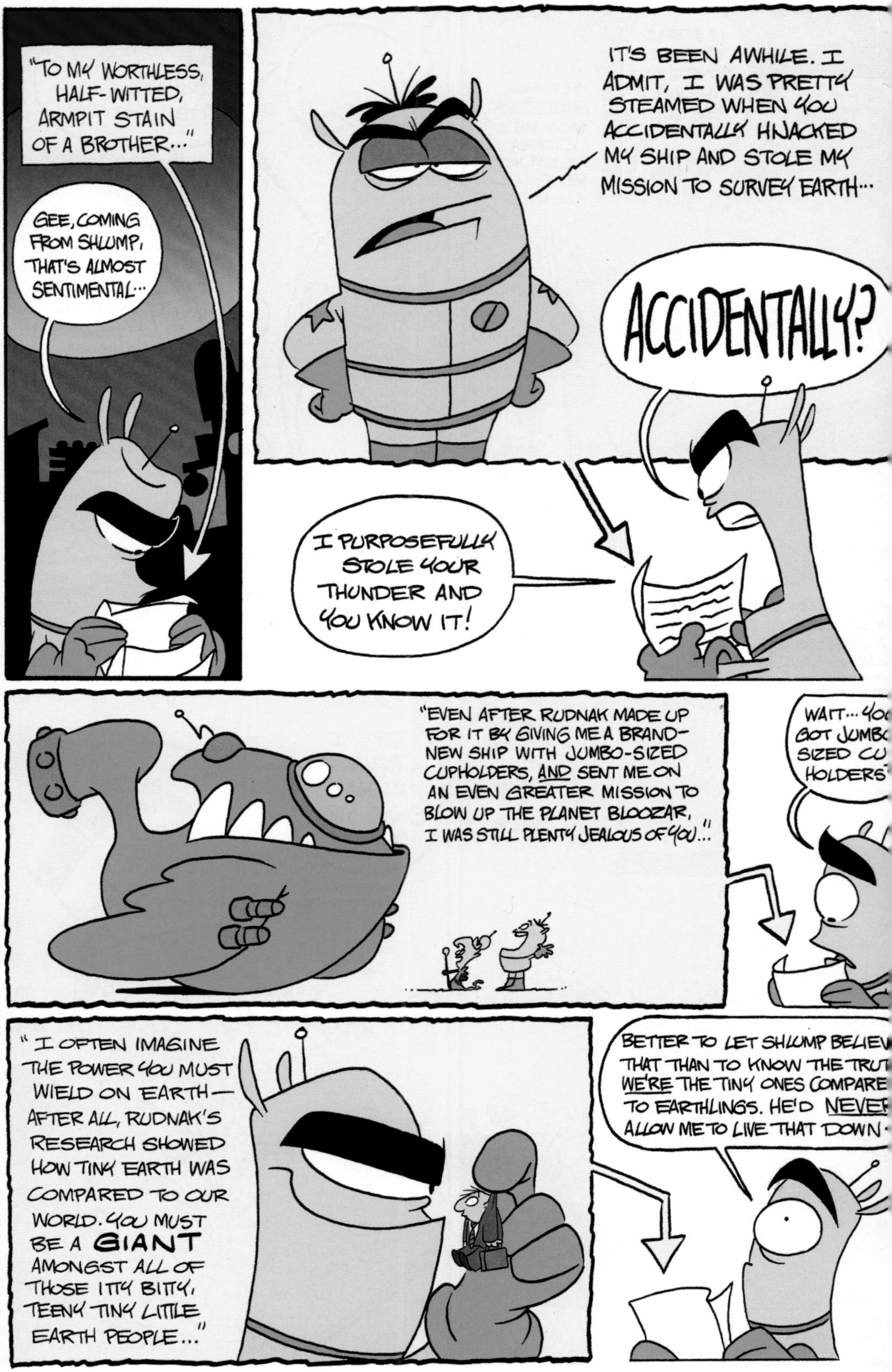
"TO MY WORTHLESS, HALF-WITTED, ARMPIT STAIN OF A BROTHER..."
GEE, COMING FROM SHLUMP, THAT'S ALMOST SENTIMENTAL...
IT'S BEEN AWHILE. I ADMIT, I WAS PRETTY STEAMED WHEN YOU ACCIDENTALLY HIJACKED MY SHIP AND STOLE MY MISSION TO SURVEY EARTH...
ACCIDENTALLY?
I PURPOSEFULLY STOLE YOUR THUNDER AND YOU KNOW IT!
"EVEN AFTER RUDNAK MADE UP FOR IT BY GIVING ME A BRAND-NEW SHIP WITH JUMBO-SIZED CUPHOLDERS, AND SENT ME ON AN EVEN GREATER MISSION TO BLOW UP THE PLANET BLOOZAR, I WAS STILL PLENTY JEALOUS OF YOU..."
"I OFTEN IMAGINE THE POWER YOU MUST WIELD ON EARTH— AFTER ALL, RUDNAK'S RESEARCH SHOWED HOW TINY EARTH WAS COMPARED TO OUR WORLD. YOU MUST BE A GIANT AMONGST ALL OF THOSE ITTY BITTY, TEENY TINY LITTLE EARTH PEOPLE..."

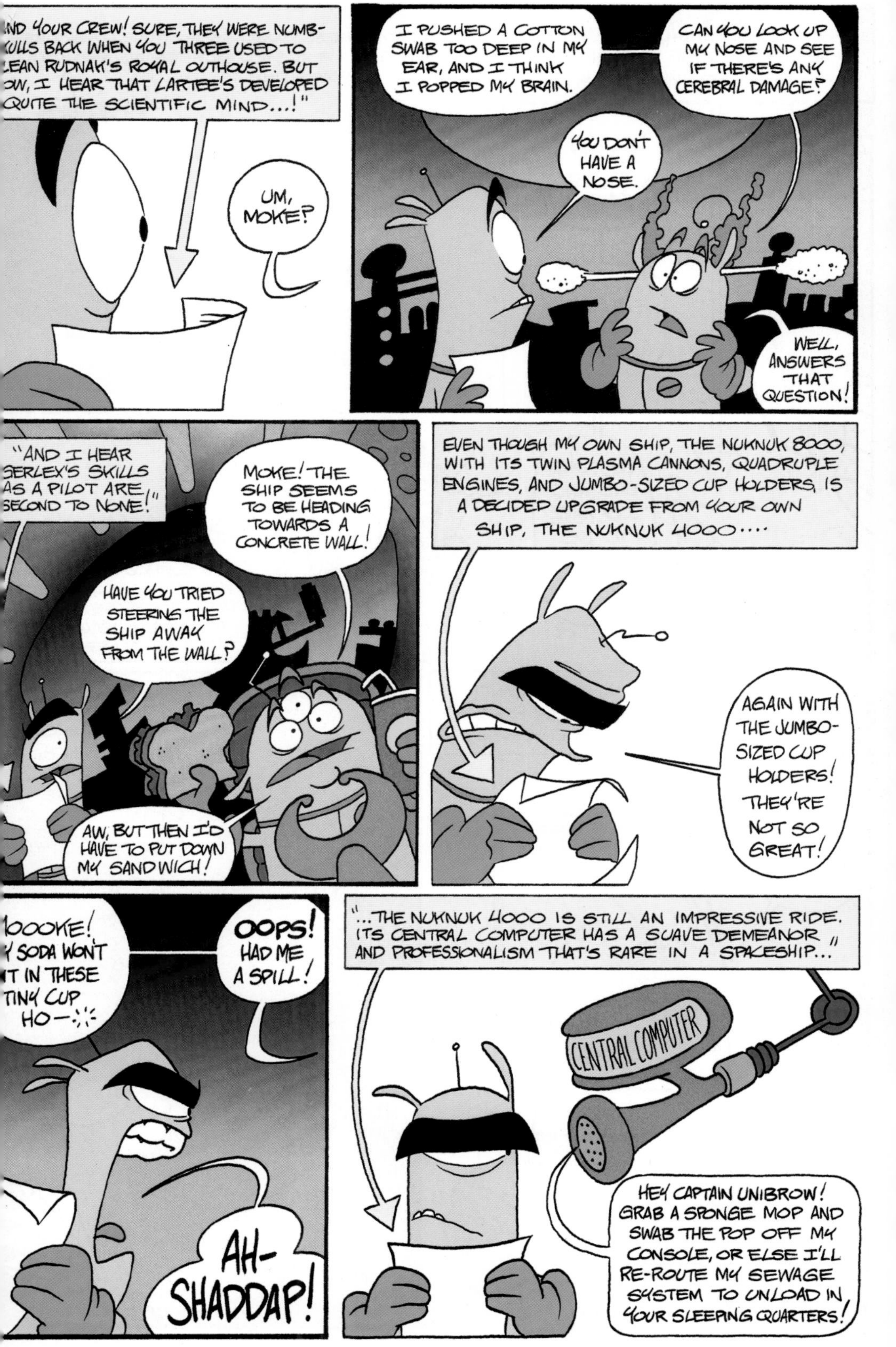
ND YOUR CREW! SURE, THEY WERE NUMB-
KULLS BACK WHEN YOU THREE USED TO
LEAN RUDNAK'S ROYAL OUTHOUSE. BUT
OW, I HEAR THAT LARTEE'S DEVELOPED
QUITE THE SCIENTIFIC MIND...!"
UM, MOKE?
I PUSHED A COTTON SWAB TOO DEEP IN MY EAR, AND I THINK I POPPED MY BRAIN.
CAN YOU LOOK UP MY NOSE AND SEE IF THERE'S ANY CEREBRAL DAMAGE?
YOU DON'T HAVE A NOSE.
WELL, ANSWERS THAT QUESTION!
"AND I HEAR
SERLEX'S SKILLS
AS A PILOT ARE
SECOND TO NONE!"
MOKE! THE SHIP SEEMS TO BE HEADING TOWARDS A CONCRETE WALL!
HAVE YOU TRIED STEERING THE SHIP AWAY FROM THE WALL?
AW, BUT THEN I'D HAVE TO PUT DOWN MY SANDWICH!
EVEN THOUGH MY OWN SHIP, THE NUKNUK 8000, WITH ITS TWIN PLASMA CANNONS, QUADRUPLE ENGINES, AND JUMBO-SIZED CUP HOLDERS, IS A DECIDED UPGRADE FROM YOUR OWN SHIP, THE NUKNUK 4000....
AGAIN WITH THE JUMBO-SIZED CUP HOLDERS! THEY'RE NOT SO GREAT!
OOOOKE!
Y SODA WON'T
T IN THESE
TINY CUP
HO—
OOPS! HAD ME A SPILL!
AH-SHADDAP!
"...THE NUKNUK 4000 IS STILL AN IMPRESSIVE RIDE. ITS CENTRAL COMPUTER HAS A SUAVE DEMEANOR AND PROFESSIONALISM THAT'S RARE IN A SPACESHIP..."
CENTRAL COMPUTER
HEY CAPTAIN UNIBROW! GRAB A SPONGE MOP AND SWAB THE POP OFF MY CONSOLE, OR ELSE I'LL RE-ROUTE MY SEWAGE SYSTEM TO UNLOAD IN YOUR SLEEPING QUARTERS!

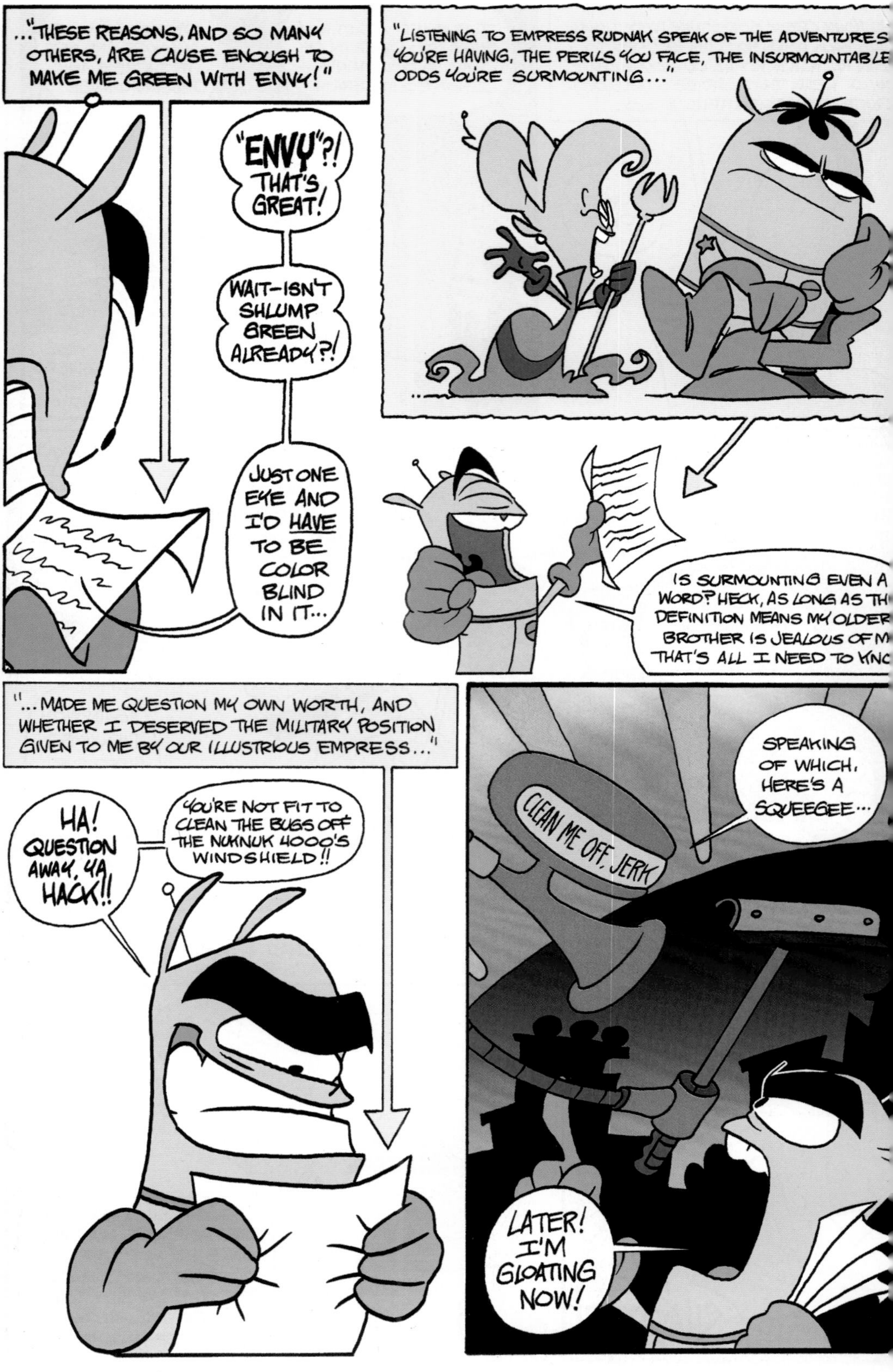
..."THESE REASONS, AND SO MANY OTHERS, ARE CAUSE ENOUGH TO MAKE ME GREEN WITH ENVY!"
"ENVY"?! THAT'S GREAT!
WAIT-ISN'T SHLUMP GREEN ALREADY?!
JUST ONE EYE AND I'D HAVE TO BE COLOR BLIND IN IT...
"LISTENING TO EMPRESS RUDNAK SPEAK OF THE ADVENTURES YOU'RE HAVING, THE PERILS YOU FACE, THE INSURMOUNTABLE ODDS YOU'RE SURMOUNTING..."
IS SURMOUNTING EVEN A WORD? HECK, AS LONG AS TH DEFINITION MEANS MY OLDER BROTHER IS JEALOUS OF M THAT'S ALL I NEED TO KNO
"...MADE ME QUESTION MY OWN WORTH, AND WHETHER I DESERVED THE MILITARY POSITION GIVEN TO ME BY OUR ILLUSTRIOUS EMPRESS..."
HA! QUESTION AWAY, YA HACK!!
YOU'RE NOT FIT TO CLEAN THE BUGS OFF THE NUKNUK 4000'S WINDSHIELD!!
CLEAN ME OFF, JERK
SPEAKING OF WHICH, HERE'S A SQUEEGEE...
LATER! I'M GLOATING NOW!

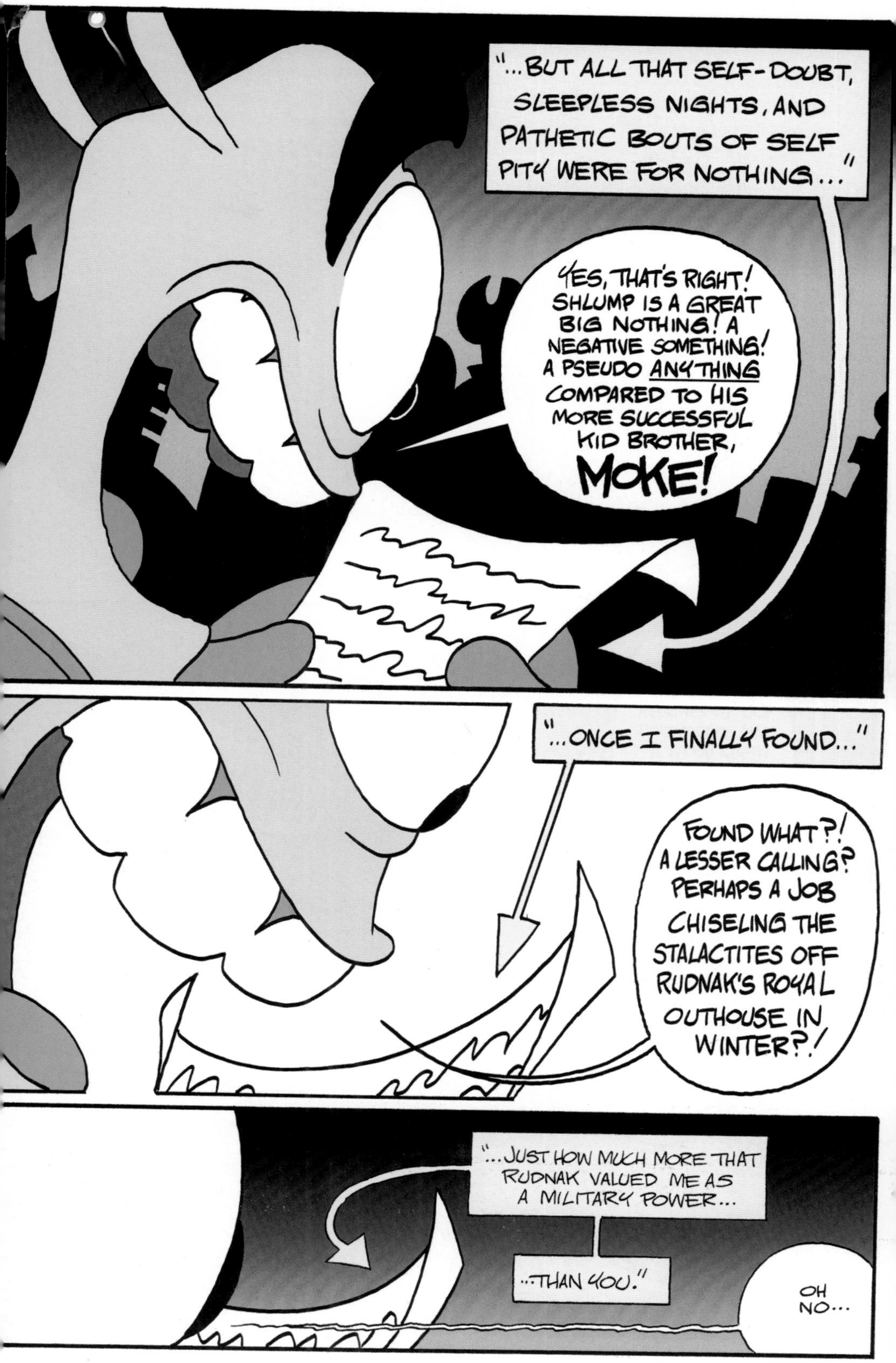
"...BUT ALL THAT SELF-DOUBT, SLEEPLESS NIGHTS, AND PATHETIC BOUTS OF SELF PITY WERE FOR NOTHING..."
YES, THAT'S RIGHT! SHLUMP IS A GREAT BIG NOTHING! A NEGATIVE SOMETHING! A PSEUDO ANYTHING COMPARED TO HIS MORE SUCCESSFUL KID BROTHER, MOKE!
"...ONCE I FINALLY FOUND..."
FOUND WHAT?! A LESSER CALLING? PERHAPS A JOB CHISELING THE STALACTITES OFF RUDNAK'S ROYAL OUTHOUSE IN WINTER?!
"...JUST HOW MUCH MORE THAT RUDNAK VALUED ME AS A MILITARY POWER...
...THAN YOU."
OH NO...

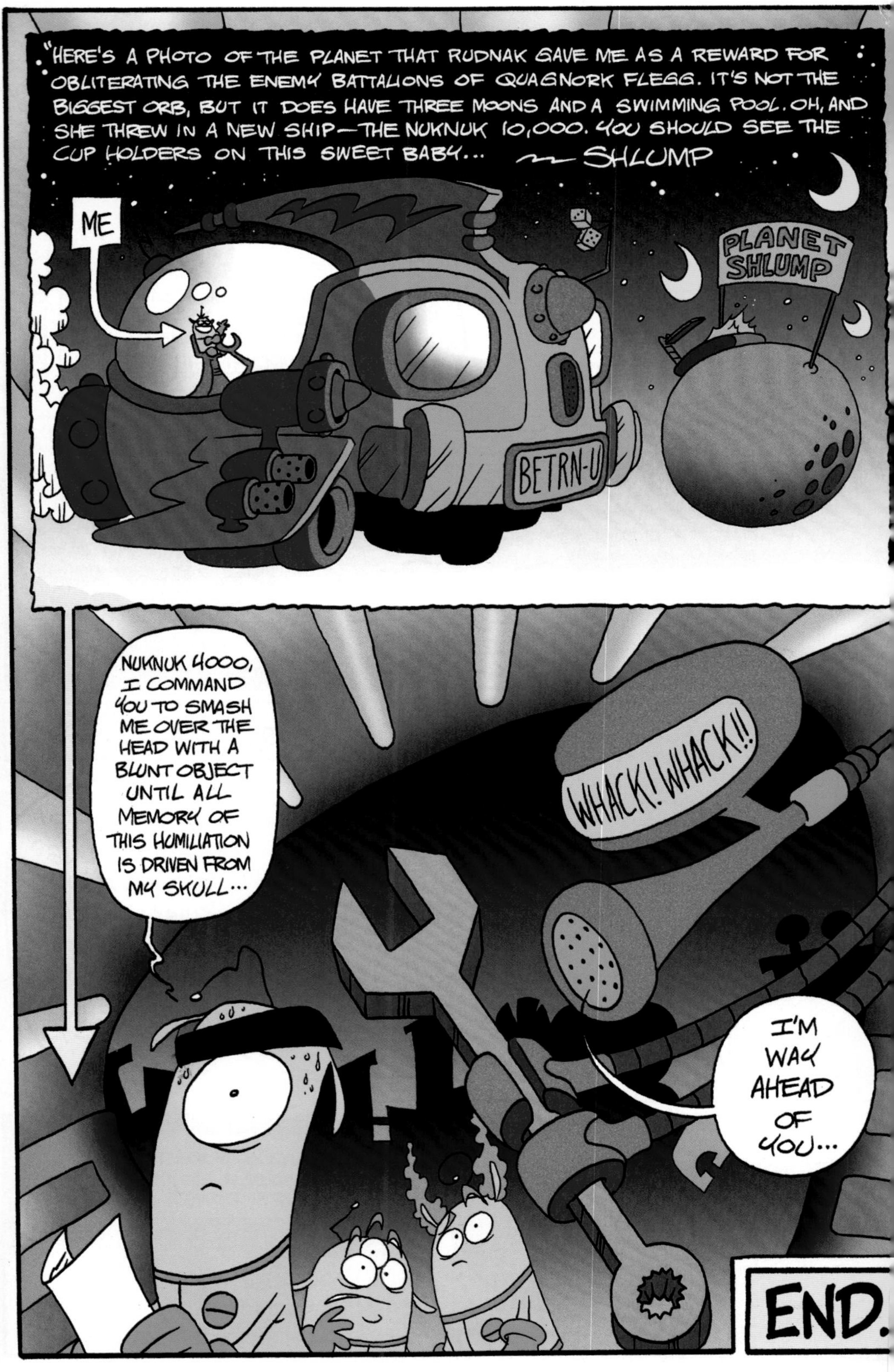
"HERE'S A PHOTO OF THE PLANET THAT RUDNAK GAVE ME AS A REWARD FOR OBLITERATING THE ENEMY BATTALIONS OF QUAGNORK FLEGG. IT'S NOT THE BIGGEST ORB, BUT IT DOES HAVE THREE MOONS AND A SWIMMING POOL. OH, AND SHE THREW IN A NEW SHIP—THE NUKNUK 10,000. YOU SHOULD SEE THE CUP HOLDERS ON THIS SWEET BABY... — SHLUMP
ME
PLANET SHLUMP
BETRN-U
NUKNUK 4000, I COMMAND YOU TO SMASH ME OVER THE HEAD WITH A BLUNT OBJECT UNTIL ALL MEMORY OF THIS HUMILIATION IS DRIVEN FROM MY SKULL...
WHACK! WHACK!!
I'M WAY AHEAD OF YOU...
END.

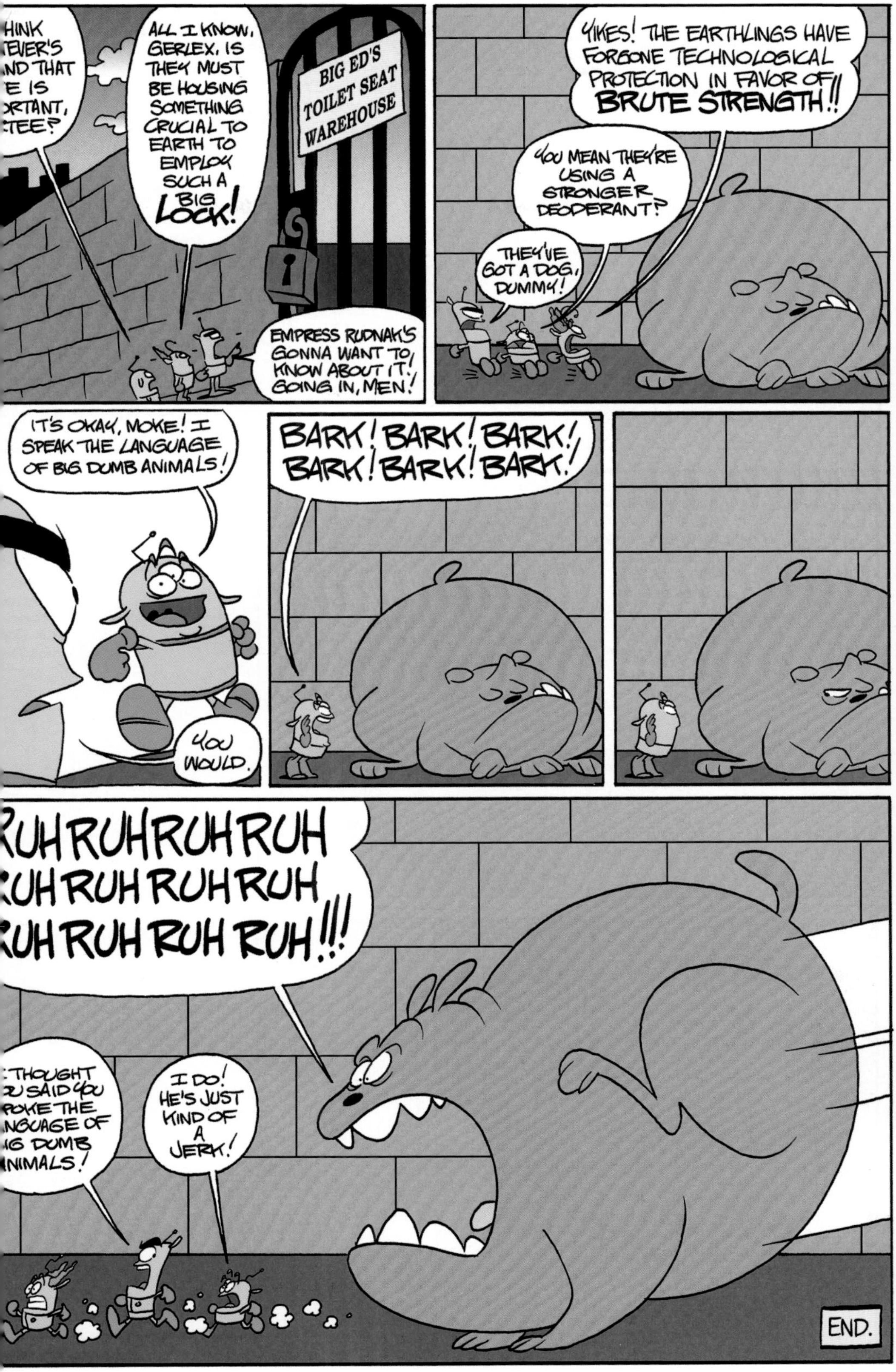

HINK
TEVER'S
IND THAT
E IS
ORTANT,
TEE?
ALL I KNOW, GERLEX, IS THEY MUST BE HOUSING SOMETHING CRUCIAL TO EARTH TO EMPLOY SUCH A BIG LOCK!
BIG ED'S TOILET SEAT WAREHOUSE
EMPRESS RUDNAK'S GONNA WANT TO KNOW ABOUT IT. GOING IN, MEN!
YIKES! THE EARTHLINGS HAVE FORGONE TECHNOLOGICAL PROTECTION IN FAVOR OF BRUTE STRENGTH!!
YOU MEAN THEY'RE USING A STRONGER DEODERANT?
THEY'VE GOT A DOG, DUMMY!
IT'S OKAY, MOKE! I SPEAK THE LANGUAGE OF BIG DUMB ANIMALS!
YOU WOULD.
BARK! BARK! BARK! BARK! BARK! BARK!
RUH RUH RUH RUH
RUH RUH RUH RUH
RUH RUH RUH RUH!!!
I THOUGHT
OU SAID YOU
POKE THE
NGUAGE OF
IG DUMB
NIMALS!
I DO! HE'S JUST KIND OF A JERK!
END.

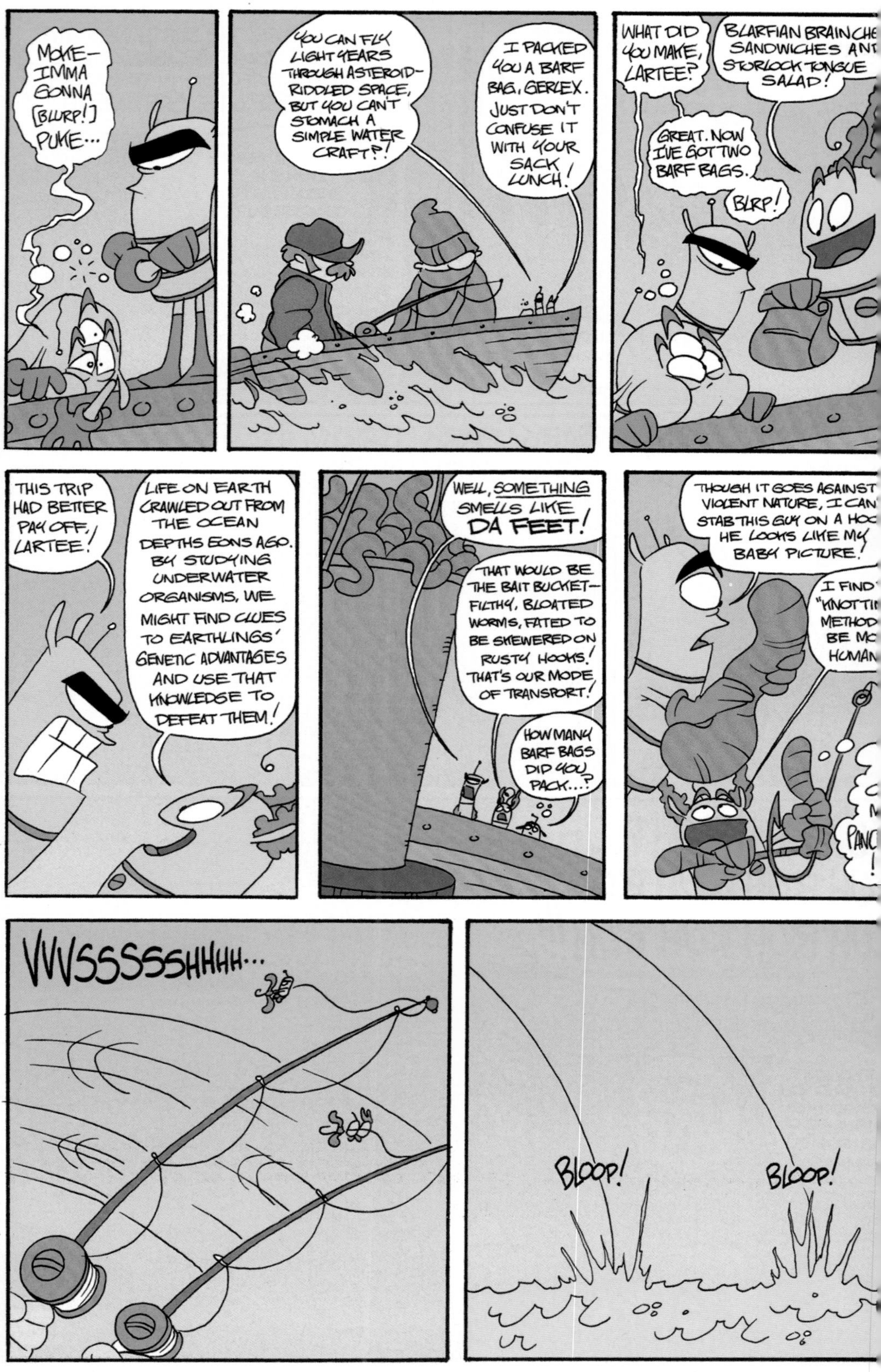
MOKE-IMMA GONNA [BLURP!] PUKE...
YOU CAN FLY LIGHT YEARS THROUGH ASTEROID-RIDDLED SPACE, BUT YOU CAN'T STOMACH A SIMPLE WATER CRAFT?!
I PACKED YOU A BARF BAG, GERLEX. JUST DON'T CONFUSE IT WITH YOUR SACK LUNCH!
WHAT DID YOU MAKE, LARTEE?
BLARFIAN BRAIN CHE SANDWICHES AN STORLOCK TONGUE SALAD!
GREAT. NOW I'VE GOT TWO BARF BAGS.
BLRP!
THIS TRIP HAD BETTER PAY OFF, LARTEE!
LIFE ON EARTH CRAWLED OUT FROM THE OCEAN DEPTHS EONS AGO. BY STUDYING UNDERWATER ORGANISMS, WE MIGHT FIND CLUES TO EARTHLINGS' GENETIC ADVANTAGES AND USE THAT KNOWLEDGE TO DEFEAT THEM!
WELL, SOMETHING SMELLS LIKE DA FEET!
THAT WOULD BE THE BAIT BUCKET-- FILTHY, BLOATED WORMS, FATED TO BE SKEWERED ON RUSTY HOOKS! THAT'S OUR MODE OF TRANSPORT!
HOW MANY BARF BAGS DID YOU PACK...?
THOUGH IT GOES AGAINST VIOLENT NATURE, I CAN STAB THIS GUY ON A HOO HE LOOKS LIKE MY BABY PICTURE!
I FIND "KNOTTI METHOD BE MO HUMAN
VVVSSSSSSHHHH...
BLOOP!
BLOOP!

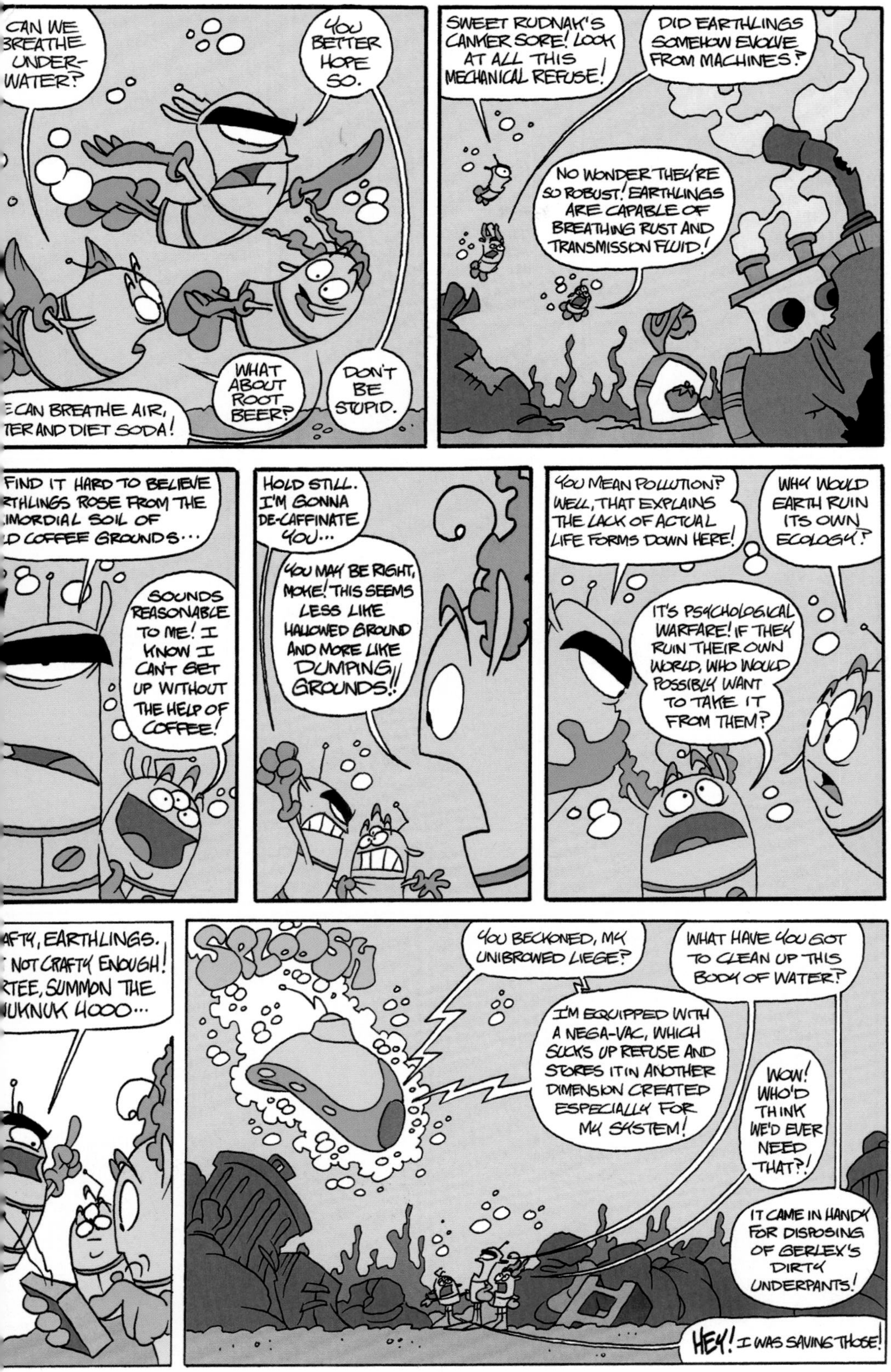
CAN WE BREATHE UNDER-WATER?
YOU BETTER HOPE SO.
E CAN BREATHE AIR, TER AND DIET SODA!
WHAT ABOUT ROOT BEER?
DON'T BE STUPID.
SWEET RUDNAK'S CANKER SORE! LOOK AT ALL THIS MECHANICAL REFUSE!
DID EARTHLINGS SOMEHOW EVOLVE FROM MACHINES?
NO WONDER THEY'RE SO ROBUST! EARTHLINGS ARE CAPABLE OF BREATHING RUST AND TRANSMISSION FLUID!
FIND IT HARD TO BELIEVE RTHLINGS ROSE FROM THE IMORDIAL SOIL OF D COFFEE GROUNDS...
SOUNDS REASONABLE TO ME! I KNOW I CAN'T GET UP WITHOUT THE HELP OF COFFEE!
HOLD STILL. I'M GONNA DE-CAFFINATE YOU...
YOU MAY BE RIGHT, MOKE! THIS SEEMS LESS LIKE HALLOWED GROUND AND MORE LIKE DUMPING GROUNDS!!
YOU MEAN POLLUTION? WELL, THAT EXPLAINS THE LACK OF ACTUAL LIFE FORMS DOWN HERE!
WHY WOULD EARTH RUIN ITS OWN ECOLOGY?
IT'S PSYCHOLOGICAL WARFARE! IF THEY RUIN THEIR OWN WORLD, WHO WOULD POSSIBLY WANT TO TAKE IT FROM THEM?
AFTY, EARTHLINGS. T NOT CRAFTY ENOUGH! RTEE, SUMMON THE UKNUK 4000...
SPLOOSH
YOU BECKONED, MY UNIBROWED LIEGE?
WHAT HAVE YOU GOT TO CLEAN UP THIS BODY OF WATER?
I'M EQUIPPED WITH A NEGA-VAC, WHICH SUCKS UP REFUSE AND STORES IT IN ANOTHER DIMENSION CREATED ESPECIALLY FOR MY SYSTEM!
WOW! WHO'D THINK WE'D EVER NEED THAT?!
IT CAME IN HANDY FOR DISPOSING OF GERLEX'S DIRTY UNDERPANTS!
HEY! I WAS SAVING THOSE!

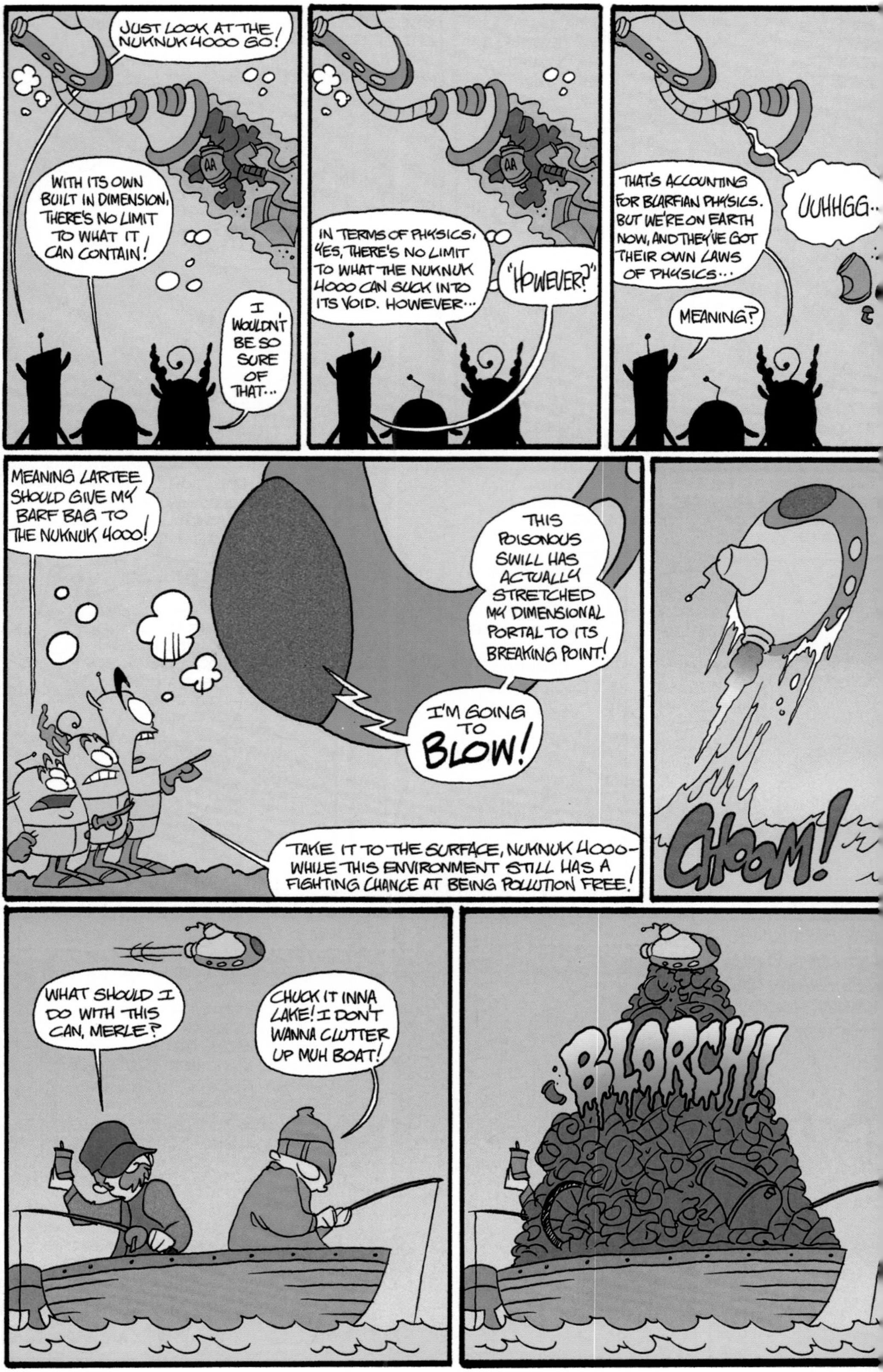
JUST LOOK AT THE NUKNUK 4000 GO!
WITH ITS OWN BUILT IN DIMENSION, THERE'S NO LIMIT TO WHAT IT CAN CONTAIN!
I WOULDN'T BE SO SURE OF THAT...
IN TERMS OF PHYSICS, YES, THERE'S NO LIMIT TO WHAT THE NUKNUK 4000 CAN SUCK INTO ITS VOID. HOWEVER...
"HOWEVER?"
THAT'S ACCOUNTING FOR BLARFIAN PHYSICS. BUT WE'RE ON EARTH NOW, AND THEY'VE GOT THEIR OWN LAWS OF PHYSICS...
UUHHGG...
MEANING?
MEANING LARTEE SHOULD GIVE MY BARF BAG TO THE NUKNUK 4000!
THIS POISONOUS SWILL HAS ACTUALLY STRETCHED MY DIMENSIONAL PORTAL TO ITS BREAKING POINT!
I'M GOING TO BLOW!
TAKE IT TO THE SURFACE, NUKNUK 4000- WHILE THIS ENVIRONMENT STILL HAS A FIGHTING CHANCE AT BEING POLLUTION FREE!
CHOOM!
WHAT SHOULD I DO WITH THIS CAN, MERLE?
CHUCK IT INNA LAKE! I DON'T WANNA CLUTTER UP MUH BOAT!
BLORCH!

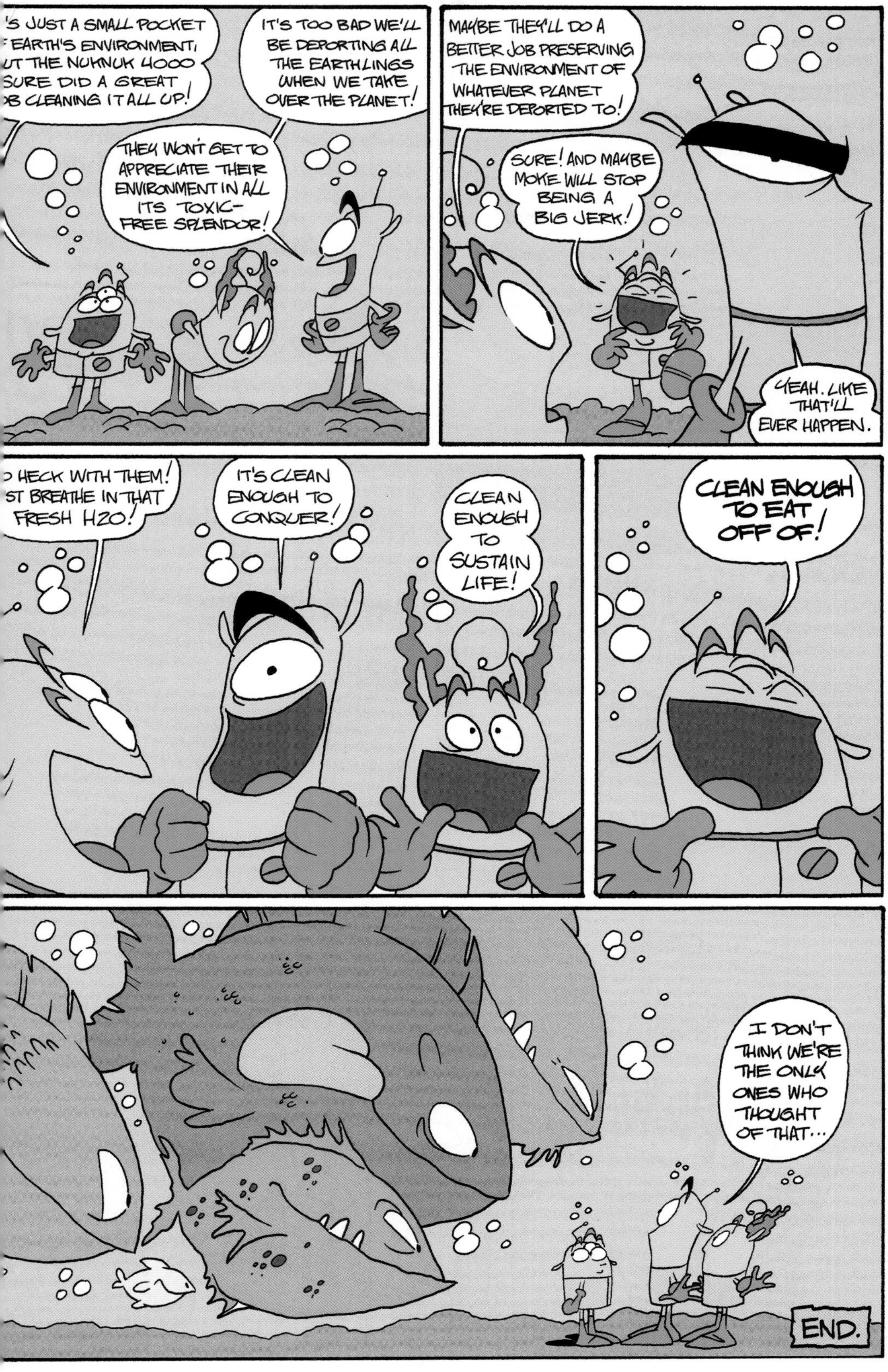
'S JUST A SMALL POCKET F EARTH'S ENVIRONMENT, UT THE NUKNUK 4000 SURE DID A GREAT OB CLEANING IT ALL UP!
IT'S TOO BAD WE'LL BE DEPORTING ALL THE EARTHLINGS WHEN WE TAKE OVER THE PLANET!
THEY WON'T GET TO APPRECIATE THEIR ENVIRONMENT IN ALL ITS TOXIC-FREE SPLENDOR!
MAYBE THEY'LL DO A BETTER JOB PRESERVING THE ENVIRONMENT OF WHATEVER PLANET THEY'RE DEPORTED TO!
SURE! AND MAYBE MOKE WILL STOP BEING A BIG JERK!
YEAH. LIKE THAT'LL EVER HAPPEN.
O HECK WITH THEM! ST BREATHE IN THAT FRESH H2O!
IT'S CLEAN ENOUGH TO CONQUER!
CLEAN ENOUGH TO SUSTAIN LIFE!
CLEAN ENOUGH TO EAT OFF OF!
I DON'T THINK WE'RE THE ONLY ONES WHO THOUGHT OF THAT...
END.

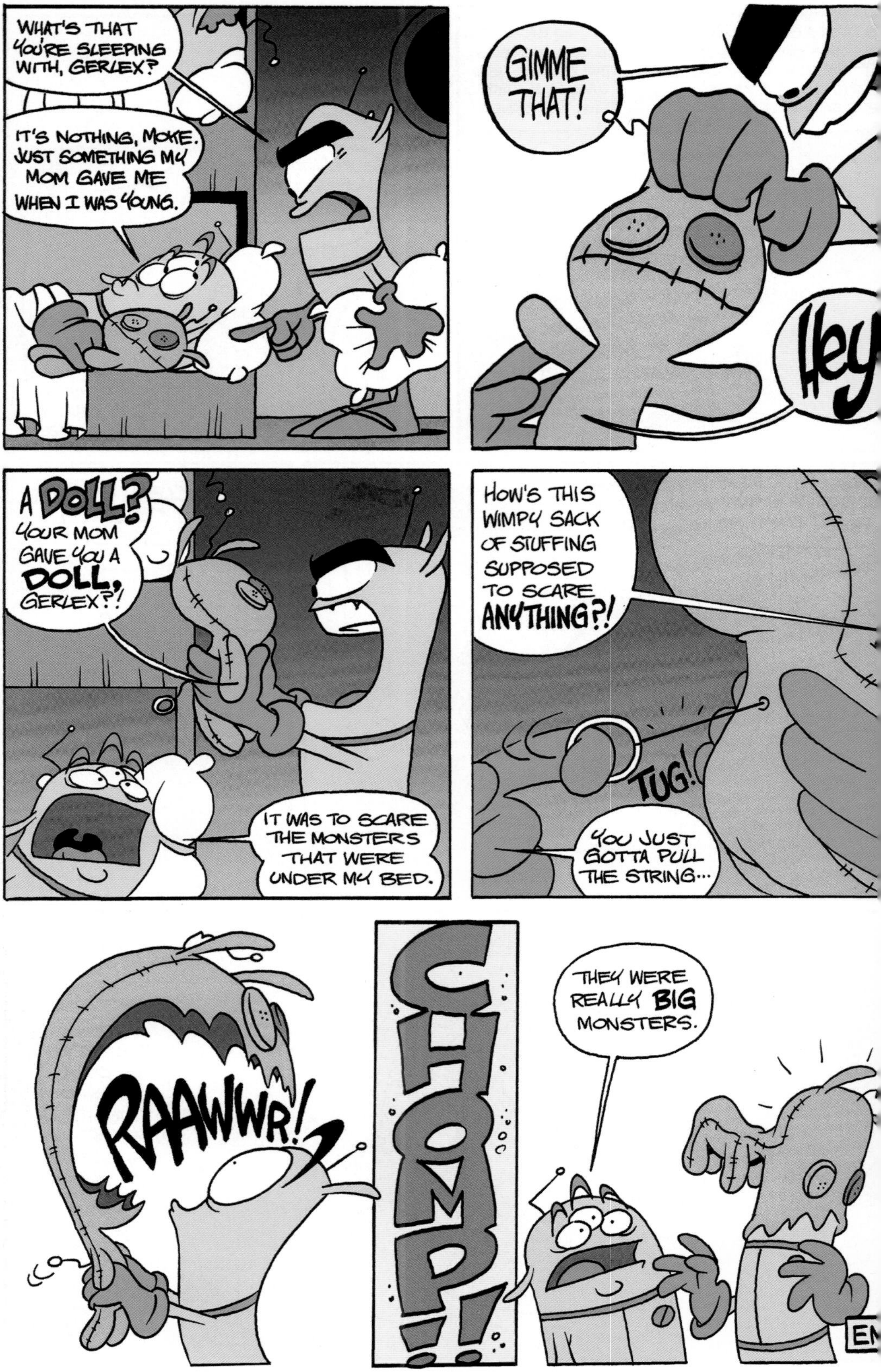

WHAT'S THAT YOU'RE SLEEPING WITH, GERLEX?
IT'S NOTHING, MOKE. JUST SOMETHING MY MOM GAVE ME WHEN I WAS YOUNG.
GIMME THAT!
HEY
A DOLL? YOUR MOM GAVE YOU A DOLL, GERLEX?!
IT WAS TO SCARE THE MONSTERS THAT WERE UNDER MY BED.
HOW'S THIS WIMPY SACK OF STUFFING SUPPOSED TO SCARE ANYTHING?!
TUG!
YOU JUST GOTTA PULL THE STRING...
RAAWWR!
CHOMP!!
THEY WERE REALLY BIG MONSTERS.

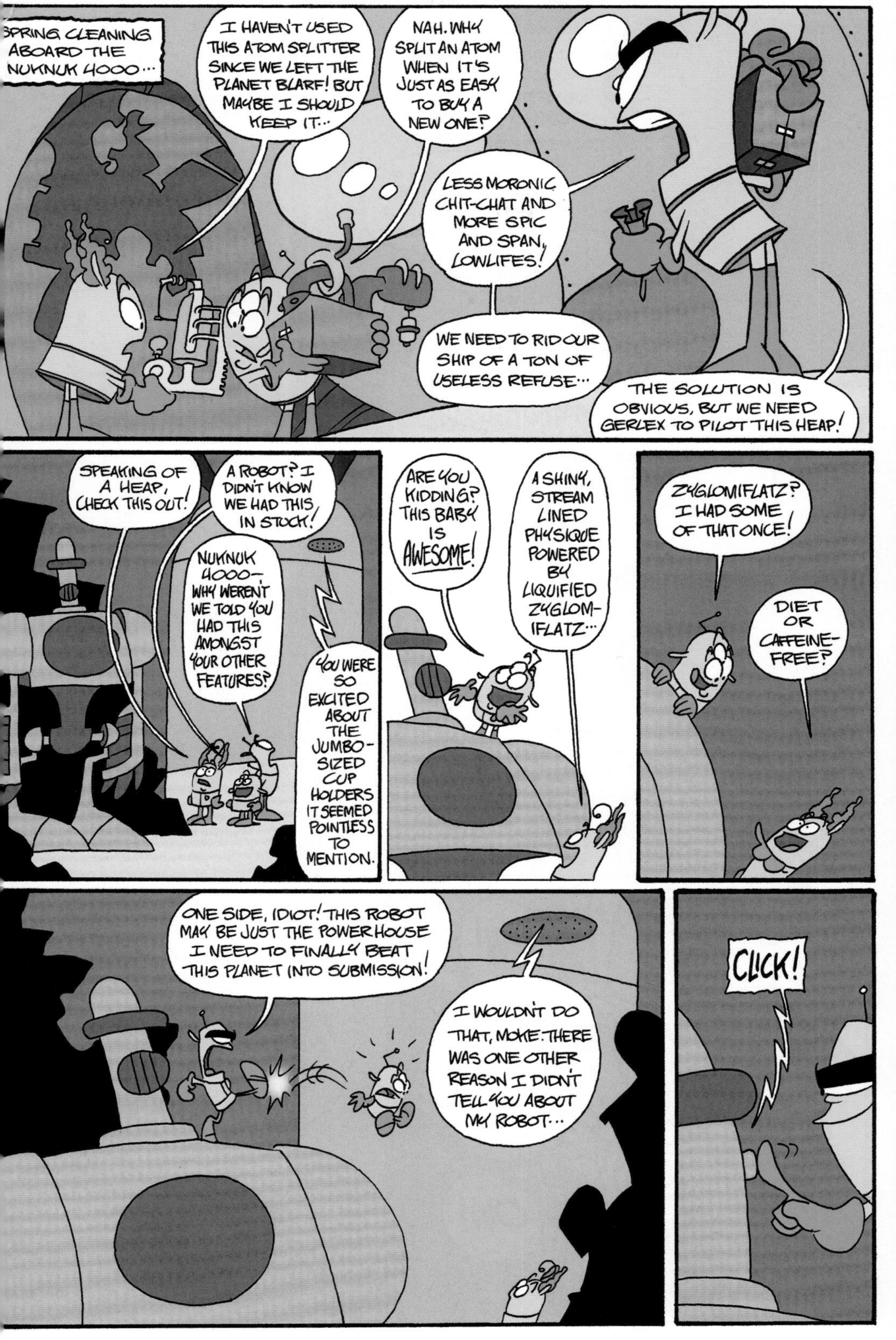

SPRING CLEANING ABOARD THE NUKNUK 4000...
I HAVEN'T USED THIS ATOM SPLITTER SINCE WE LEFT THE PLANET BLARF! BUT MAYBE I SHOULD KEEP IT...
NAH. WHY SPLIT AN ATOM WHEN IT'S JUST AS EASY TO BUY A NEW ONE?
LESS MORONIC CHIT-CHAT AND MORE SPIC AND SPAN, LOWLIFES!
WE NEED TO RID OUR SHIP OF A TON OF USELESS REFUSE...
THE SOLUTION IS OBVIOUS, BUT WE NEED GERLEX TO PILOT THIS HEAP!
SPEAKING OF A HEAP, CHECK THIS OUT!
A ROBOT? I DIDN'T KNOW WE HAD THIS IN STOCK!
NUKNUK 4000— WHY WEREN'T WE TOLD YOU HAD THIS AMONGST YOUR OTHER FEATURES?
YOU WERE SO EXCITED ABOUT THE JUMBO-SIZED CUP HOLDERS IT SEEMED POINTLESS TO MENTION.
ARE YOU KIDDING? THIS BABY IS AWESOME!
A SHINY, STREAM LINED PHYSIQUE POWERED BY LIQUIFIED ZYGLOM-IFLATZ...
ZYGLOMIFLATZ? I HAD SOME OF THAT ONCE!
DIET OR CAFFEINE-FREE?
ONE SIDE, IDIOT! THIS ROBOT MAY BE JUST THE POWER HOUSE I NEED TO FINALLY BEAT THIS PLANET INTO SUBMISSION!
I WOULDN'T DO THAT, MOKE. THERE WAS ONE OTHER REASON I DIDN'T TELL YOU ABOUT MY ROBOT...
CLICK!

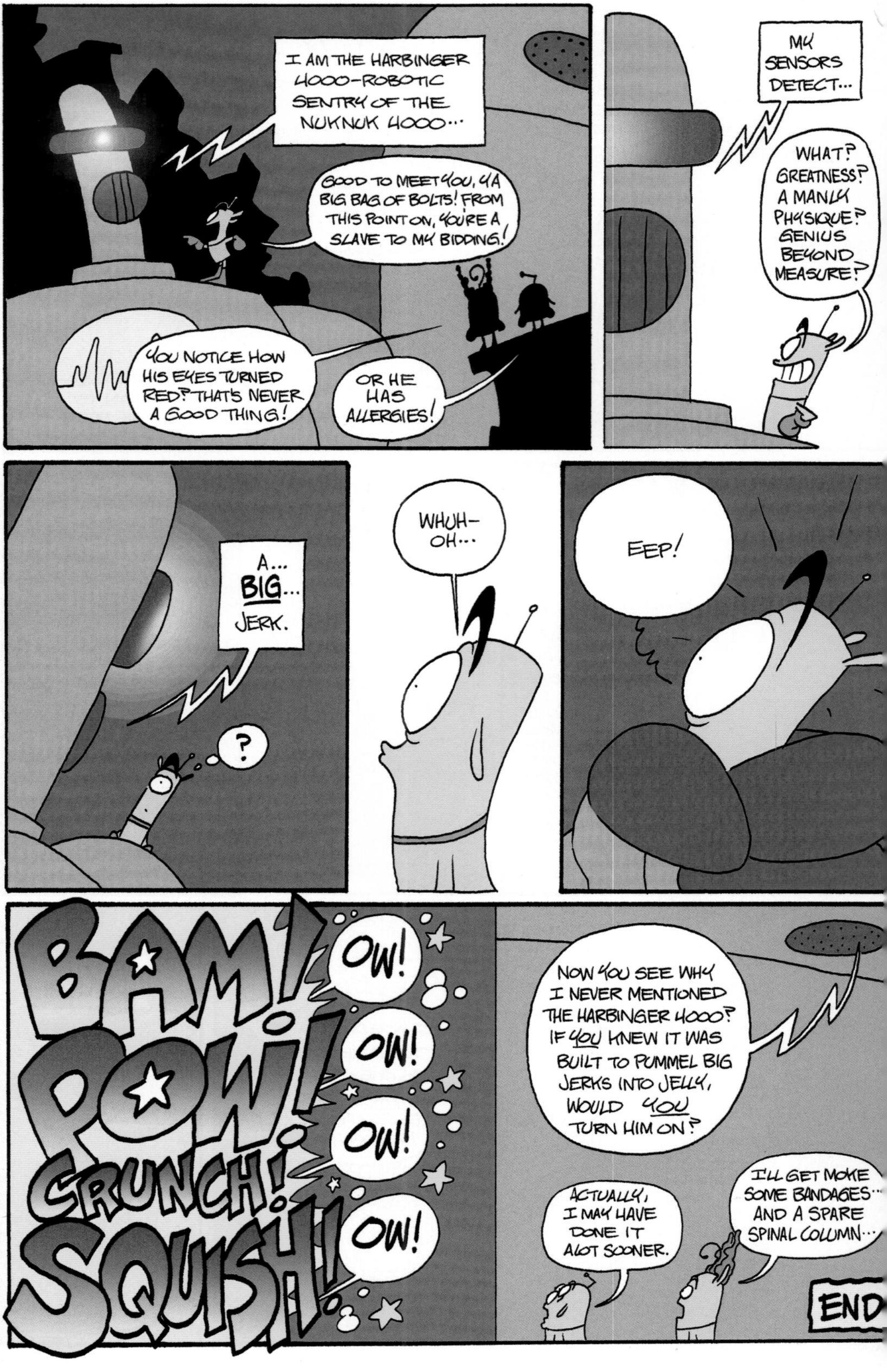
I AM THE HARBINGER 4000-ROBOTIC SENTRY OF THE NUKNUK 4000...
GOOD TO MEET YOU, YA BIG BAG OF BOLTS! FROM THIS POINT ON, YOU'RE A SLAVE TO MY BIDDING!
YOU NOTICE HOW HIS EYES TURNED RED? THAT'S NEVER A GOOD THING!
OR HE HAS ALLERGIES!
MY SENSORS DETECT...
WHAT? GREATNESS? A MANLY PHYSIQUE? GENIUS BEYOND MEASURE?
A... BIG... JERK.
?
WHUH-OH...
EEP!
BAM! POW! CRUNCH! SQUISH!
OW!
OW!
OW!
OW!
NOW YOU SEE WHY I NEVER MENTIONED THE HARBINGER 4000? IF YOU KNEW IT WAS BUILT TO PUMMEL BIG JERKS INTO JELLY, WOULD YOU TURN HIM ON?
ACTUALLY, I MAY HAVE DONE IT ALOT SOONER.
I'LL GET MOKE SOME BANDAGES... AND A SPARE SPINAL COLUMN...
END

HOW COME YOU ALWAYS GET TO USE THE HIGH-TECH WEAPONS?

BECAUSE I'M THE CAPTAIN. B. BECAUSE I'M NOT A HUGE ...T NAMED ...ERLEX!

I CAN'T HELP THAT MY NAME IS GERLEX!

SIGH...

FINE. YOU WANT A WEAPON? HERE...

OOH! WHAT IS IT?

IT'S CALLED A BOW AND ARROW. LARTEE "BORROWED" IT FROM SOME EARTH CHILDREN WHO WERE PLAYING WITH MINIATURE FIGURINES OF INDIGENOUS TRIBESMEN.

TRY NOT TO PUT YOUR EYE OUT, LUNKHEAD!

DON'T WORRY. I'VE GOT TWO SPARES!

...OW AND ARROW, HUH? ...ELL, I'M SURE IT'LL ...ME IN HANDY FOR ...OTECTION AGAINST ...EADLY ADVERSARIES...

GASP!

LIKE A GIANT BAG OF POTATO CHIPS!!

MRS. SALTY'S POTATO CHIPS

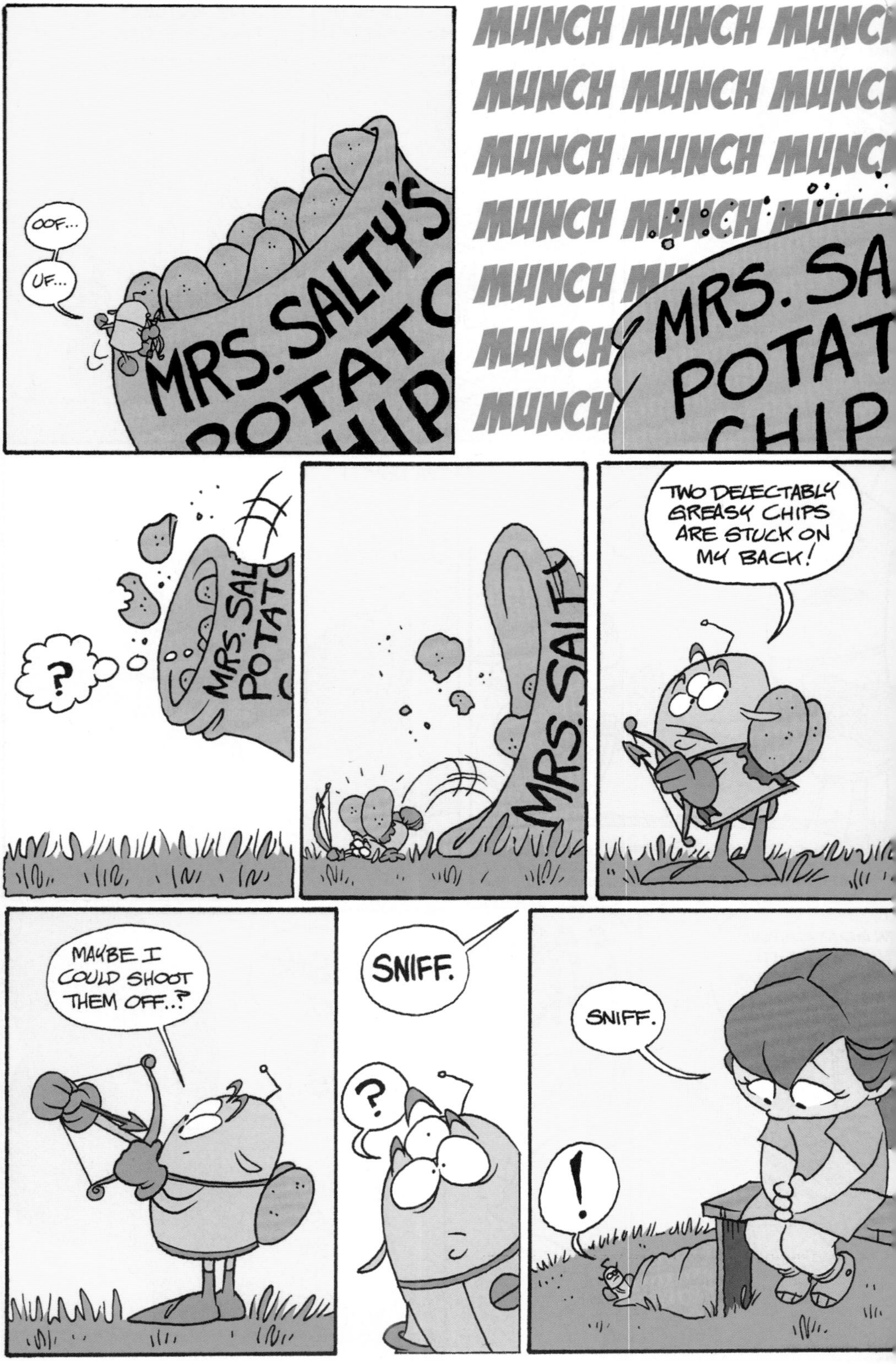

OOF...
UF...
MRS. SALTY'S POTATO CHIPS
MUNCH MUNCH MUNCH
MUNCH MUNCH MUNCH
MUNCH MUNCH MUNCH
MUNCH MUNCH MUNCH
MUNCH
MUNCH
MUNCH
MRS. SA POTAT CHIP
?
MRS. SAL POTATO
MRS. SALTY
TWO DELECTABLY GREASY CHIPS ARE STUCK ON MY BACK!
MAYBE I COULD SHOOT THEM OFF...?
SNIFF.
?
SNIFF.
!

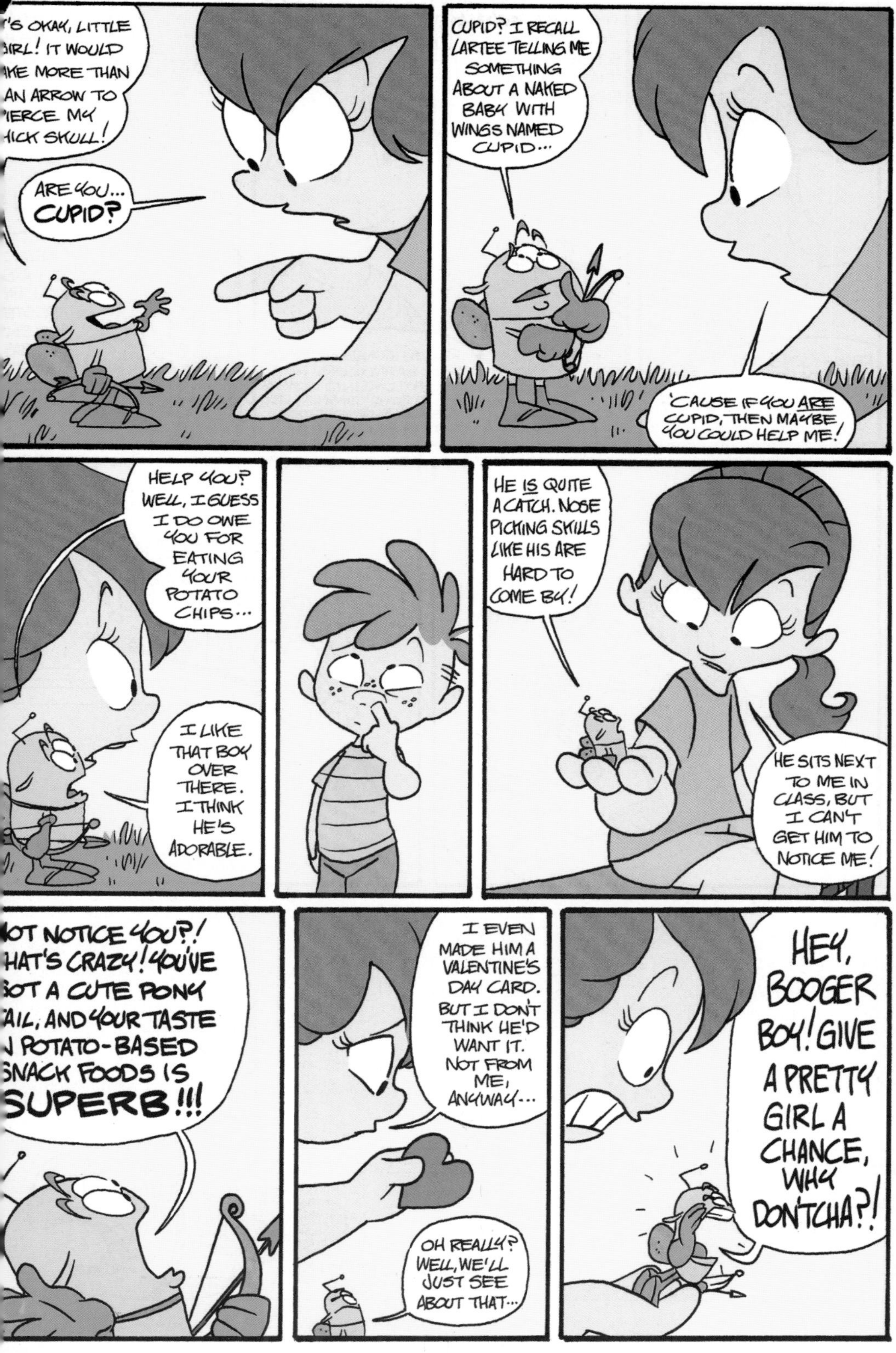

'S OKAY, LITTLE IRL! IT WOULD AKE MORE THAN AN ARROW TO IERCE MY HICK SKULL!
ARE YOU... CUPID?
CUPID? I RECALL LARTEE TELLING ME SOMETHING ABOUT A NAKED BABY WITH WINGS NAMED CUPID...
'CAUSE IF YOU ARE CUPID, THEN MAYBE YOU COULD HELP ME!
HELP YOU? WELL, I GUESS I DO OWE YOU FOR EATING YOUR POTATO CHIPS...
I LIKE THAT BOY OVER THERE. I THINK HE'S ADORABLE.
HE IS QUITE A CATCH. NOSE PICKING SKILLS LIKE HIS ARE HARD TO COME BY!
HE SITS NEXT TO ME IN CLASS, BUT I CAN'T GET HIM TO NOTICE ME!
OT NOTICE YOU?! HAT'S CRAZY! YOU'VE OT A CUTE PONY AIL, AND YOUR TASTE N POTATO-BASED NACK FOODS IS SUPERB!!!
I EVEN MADE HIM A VALENTINE'S DAY CARD. BUT I DON'T THINK HE'D WANT IT. NOT FROM ME, ANYWAY...
OH REALLY? WELL, WE'LL JUST SEE ABOUT THAT...
HEY, BOOGER BOY! GIVE A PRETTY GIRL A CHANCE, WHY DON'TCHA?!

THAT'S NOT HOW YOU'RE SUPPOSED TO DO IT!

IT'S OKAY, CUPID. YOU SEE, YOU'RE SUPPOSED TO TAKE THAT ARROW AND SHOOT HIM, MAKING HIM LIKE ME!

STI... THAT'S H... IT'S SUPPOSI... TO BE... DONE...

REALLY? I'M SORRY. I'M KINDA NEW TO THIS "GETTING BOYS TO NOTICE GIRLS" BUSINESS.

REALLY? I ONCE LAUGHED WHILE EATING CORN NUTS, AND SHOT ONE INTO MOXIE'S EYE. I DON'T THINK HE LIKED ME ANY MORE AFTER THAT. PROBABLY LESS.

WELL, I CAN'T ARGUE WITH TIME-TESTED VIOLENT LOVE-BASED EARTH RITUAL...

CREEAAAKKK....

SPROING!

WHOAH WHOAH WHOAH

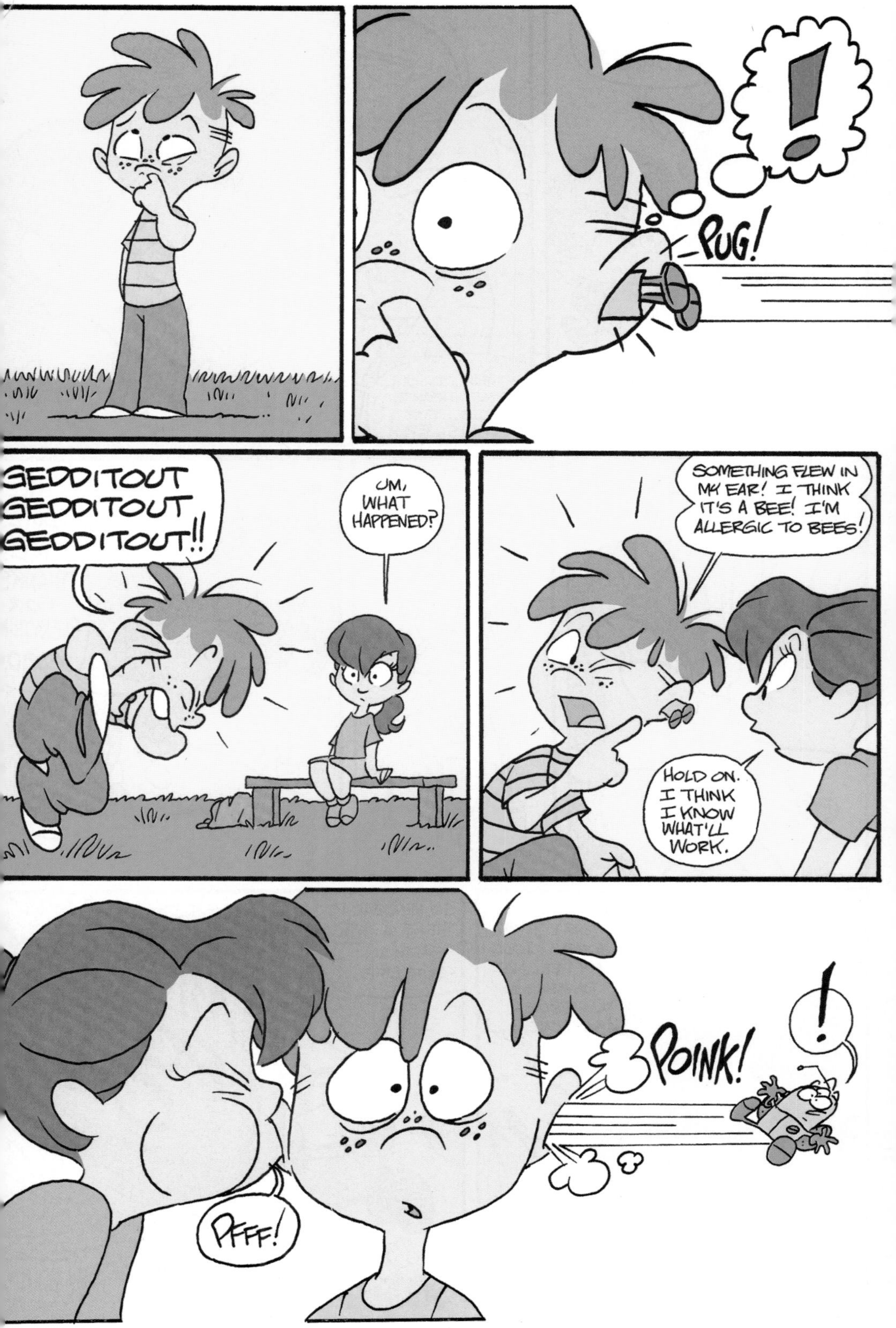
!
PUG!
GEDDITOUT GEDDITOUT GEDDITOUT!!
UM, WHAT HAPPENED?
SOMETHING FLEW IN MY EAR! I THINK IT'S A BEE! I'M ALLERGIC TO BEES!
HOLD ON. I THINK I KNOW WHAT'LL WORK.
PFFF!
POINK!
!

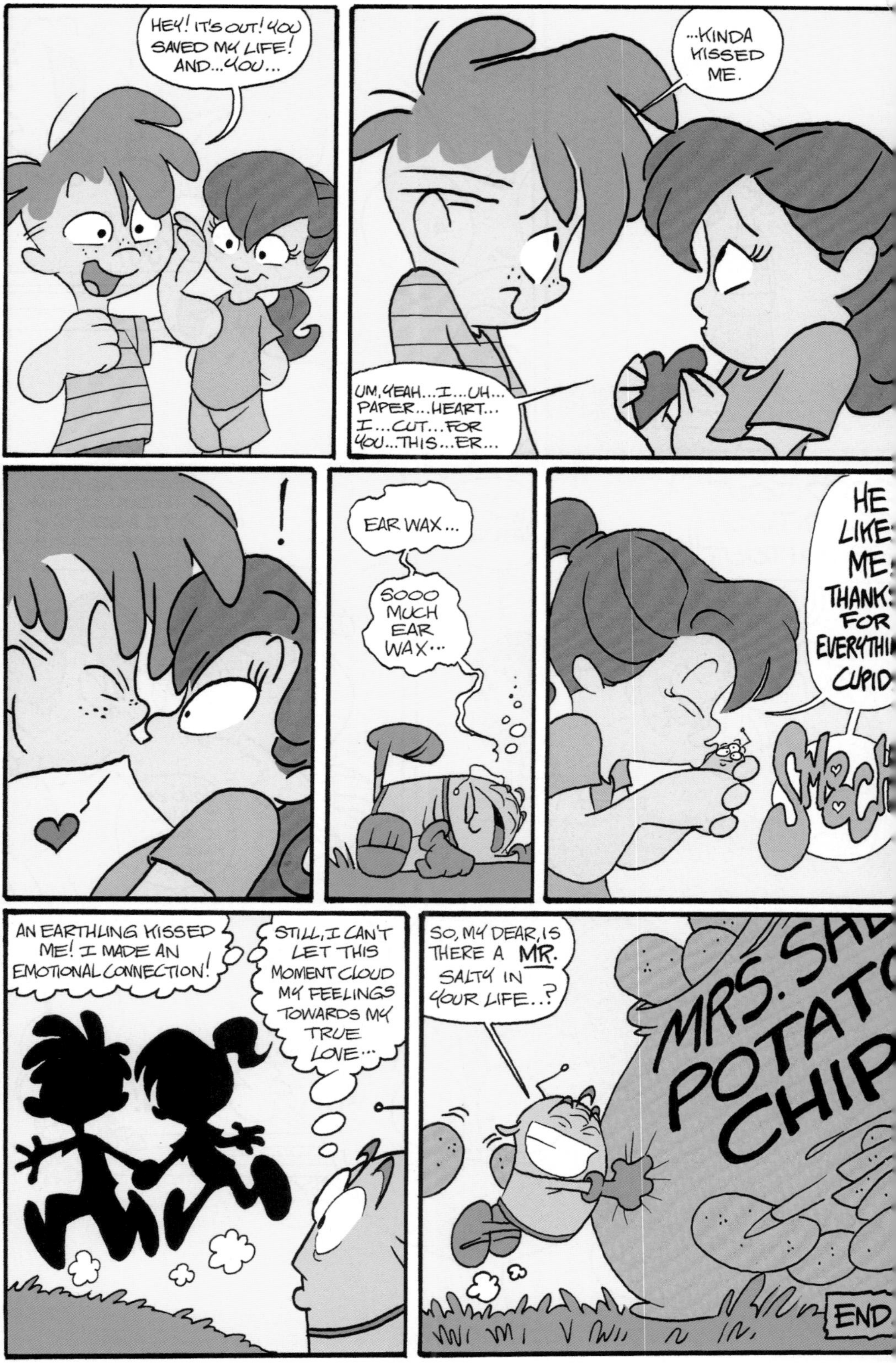
HEY! IT'S OUT! YOU SAVED MY LIFE! AND...YOU...
...KINDA KISSED ME.
UM, YEAH...I...UH... PAPER...HEART... I...CUT...FOR YOU...THIS...ER...
!
EAR WAX...
SOOO MUCH EAR WAX...
AN EARTHLING KISSED ME! I MADE AN EMOTIONAL CONNECTION!
STILL, I CAN'T LET THIS MOMENT CLOUD MY FEELINGS TOWARDS MY TRUE LOVE...
SO, MY DEAR, IS THERE A MR. SALTY IN YOUR LIFE...?
END

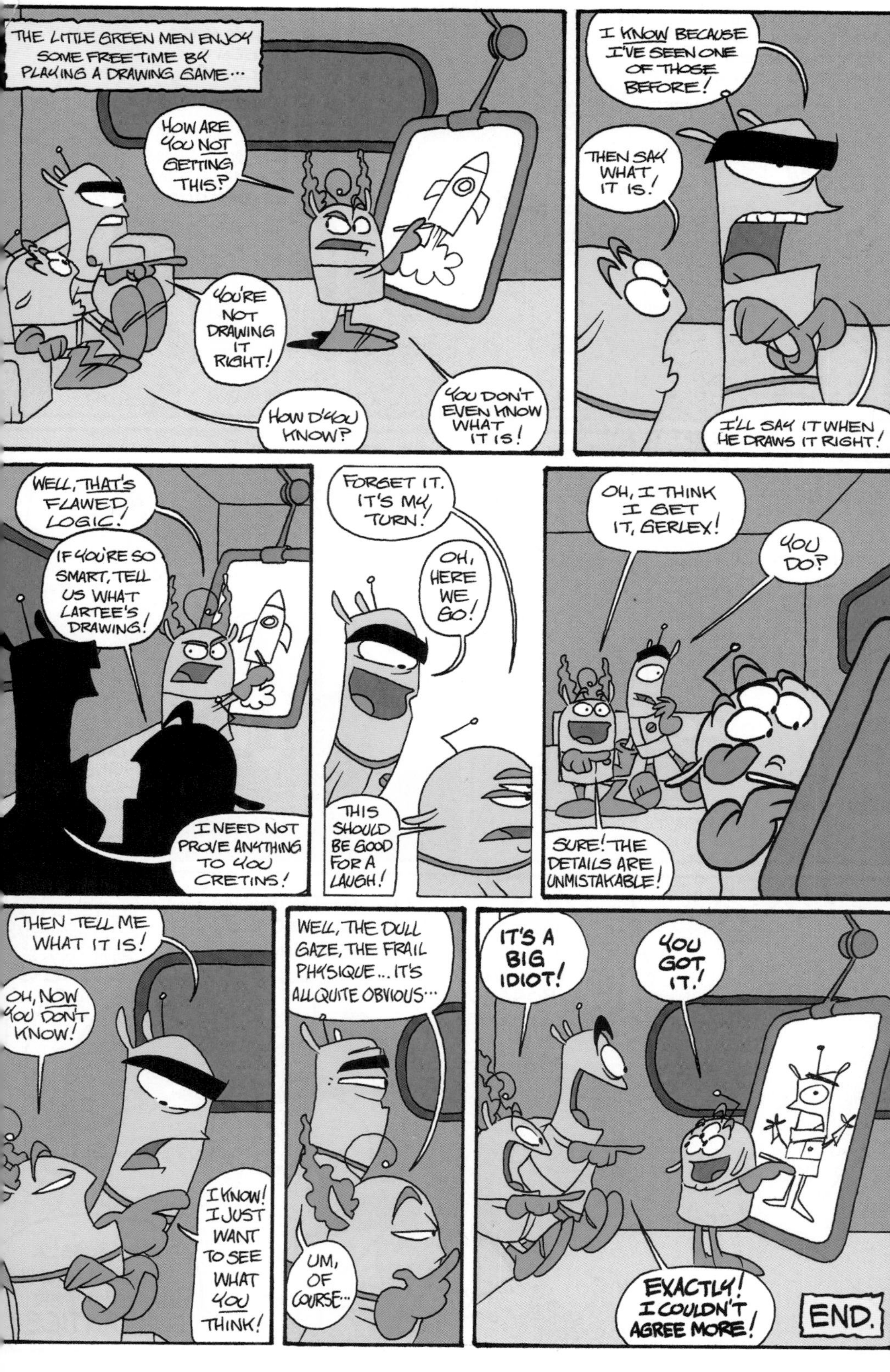
THE LITTLE GREEN MEN ENJOY SOME FREE TIME BY PLAYING A DRAWING GAME...
HOW ARE YOU NOT GETTING THIS?
YOU'RE NOT DRAWING IT RIGHT!
HOW D'YOU KNOW?
YOU DON'T EVEN KNOW WHAT IT IS!
I KNOW BECAUSE I'VE SEEN ONE OF THOSE BEFORE!
THEN SAY WHAT IT IS!
I'LL SAY IT WHEN HE DRAWS IT RIGHT!
WELL, THAT'S FLAWED LOGIC!
IF YOU'RE SO SMART, TELL US WHAT LARTEE'S DRAWING!
I NEED NOT PROVE ANYTHING TO YOU CRETINS!
FORGET IT. IT'S MY TURN!
OH, HERE WE GO!
THIS SHOULD BE GOOD FOR A LAUGH!
OH, I THINK I GET IT, GERLEX!
YOU DO?
SURE! THE DETAILS ARE UNMISTAKABLE!
THEN TELL ME WHAT IT IS!
OH, NOW YOU DON'T KNOW!
I KNOW! I JUST WANT TO SEE WHAT YOU THINK!
WELL, THE DULL GAZE, THE FRAIL PHYSIQUE... IT'S ALL QUITE OBVIOUS...
UM, OF COURSE...
IT'S A BIG IDIOT!
YOU GOT IT.
EXACTLY! I COULDN'T AGREE MORE!
END.

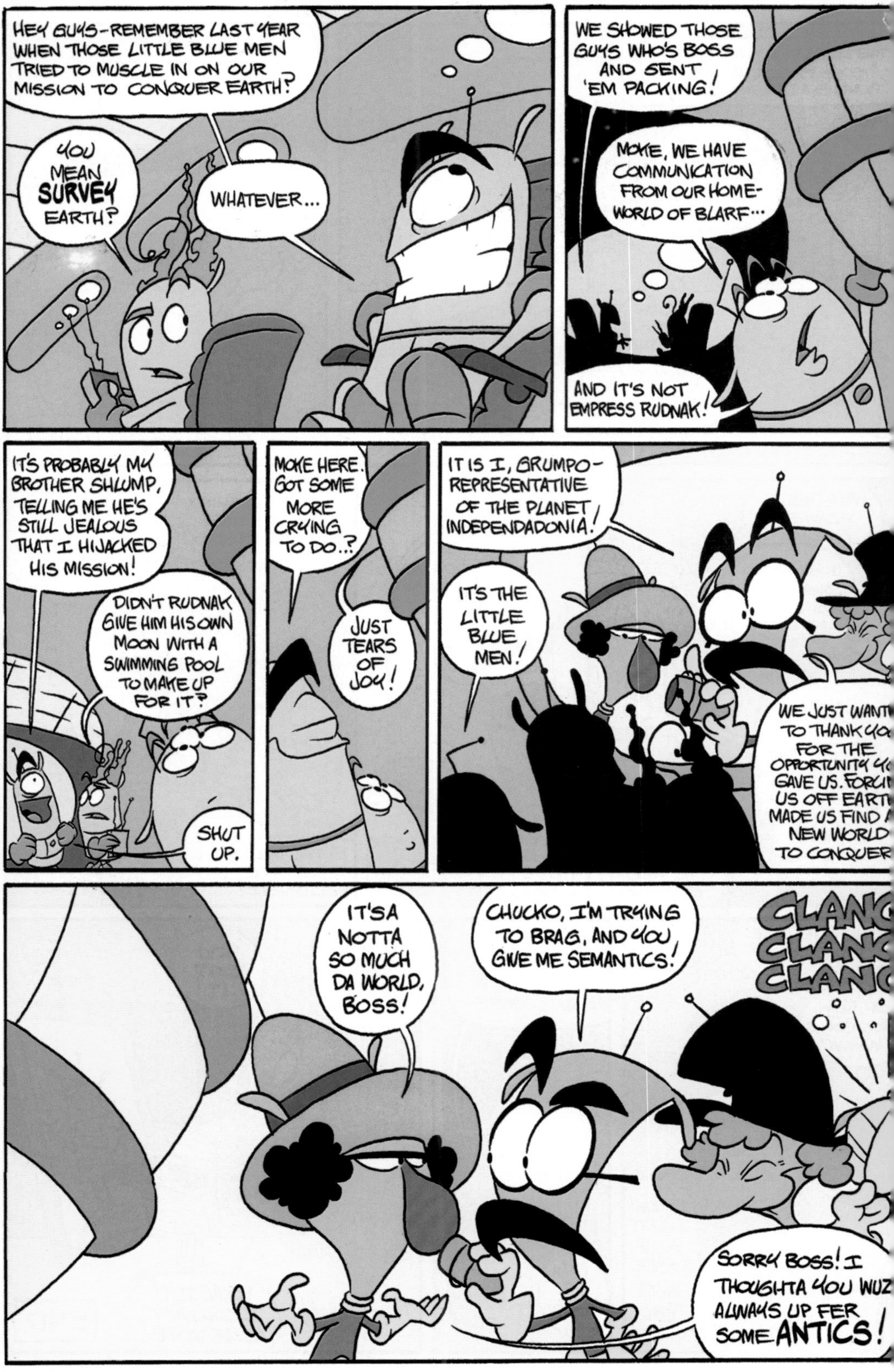
HEY GUYS-REMEMBER LAST YEAR WHEN THOSE LITTLE BLUE MEN TRIED TO MUSCLE IN ON OUR MISSION TO CONQUER EARTH?
YOU MEAN SURVEY EARTH?
WHATEVER...
WE SHOWED THOSE GUYS WHO'S BOSS AND SENT 'EM PACKING!
MOKE, WE HAVE COMMUNICATION FROM OUR HOME-WORLD OF BLARF...
AND IT'S NOT EMPRESS RUDNAK!
IT'S PROBABLY MY BROTHER SHLUMP, TELLING ME HE'S STILL JEALOUS THAT I HIJACKED HIS MISSION!
DIDN'T RUDNAK GIVE HIM HIS OWN MOON WITH A SWIMMING POOL TO MAKE UP FOR IT?
SHUT UP.
MOKE HERE. GOT SOME MORE CRYING TO DO..?
JUST TEARS OF JOY!
IT IS I, GRUMPO-REPRESENTATIVE OF THE PLANET INDEPENDADONIA!
IT'S THE LITTLE BLUE MEN!
WE JUST WANT TO THANK YO FOR THE OPPORTUNITY YO GAVE US. FORCI US OFF EART MADE US FIND A NEW WORLD TO CONQUER
IT'SA NOTTA SO MUCH DA WORLD, BOSS!
CHUCKO, I'M TRYING TO BRAG, AND YOU GIVE ME SEMANTICS!
CLANG CLANG CLANG
SORRY BOSS! I THOUGHTA YOU WUZ ALWAYS UP FER SOME ANTICS!

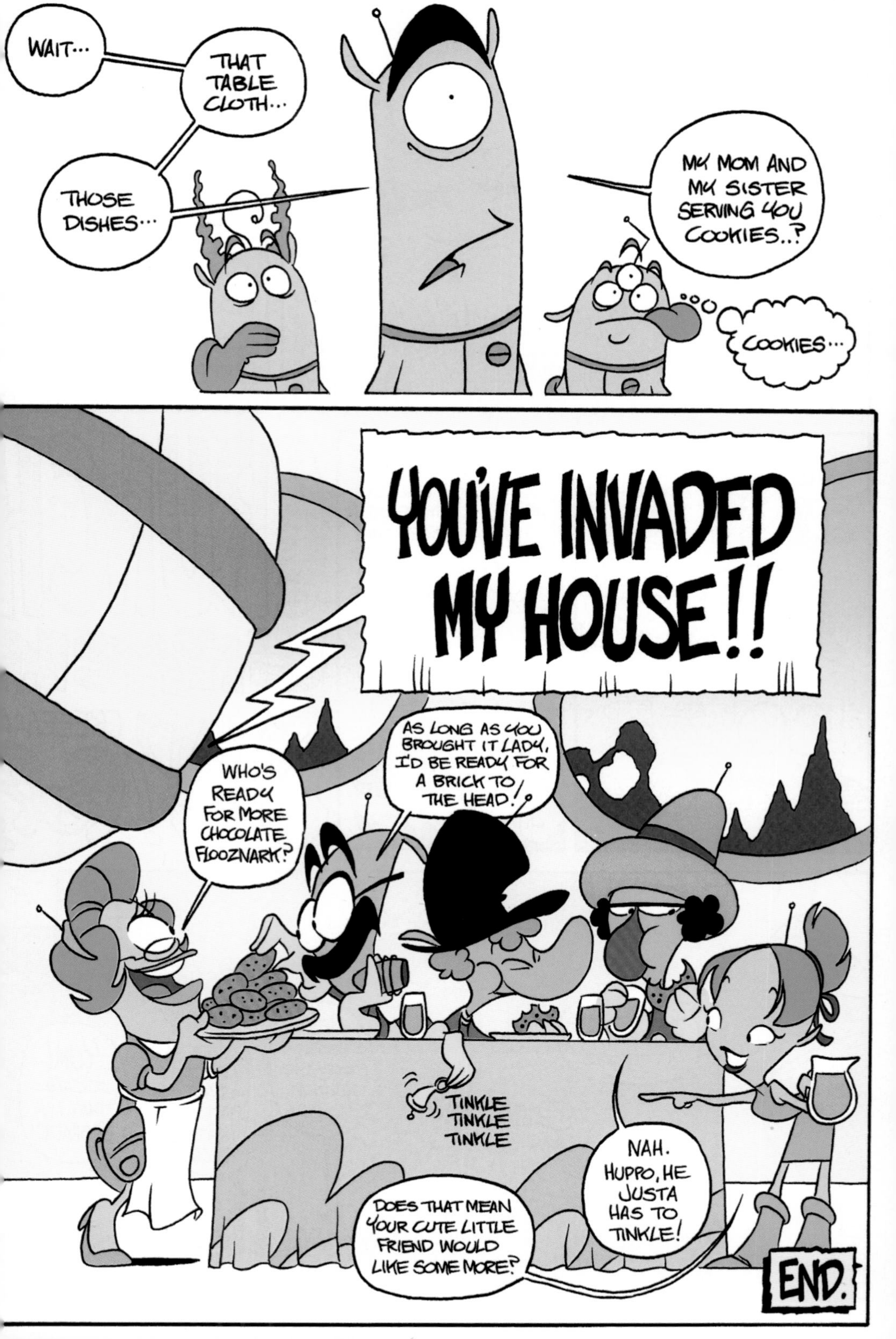
WAIT...
THAT TABLE CLOTH...
THOSE DISHES...
MY MOM AND MY SISTER SERVING YOU COOKIES...?
COOKIES...
YOU'VE INVADED MY HOUSE!!
WHO'S READY FOR MORE CHOCOLATE FLOOZNARK?
AS LONG AS YOU BROUGHT IT LADY, I'D BE READY FOR A BRICK TO THE HEAD!
TINKLE TINKLE TINKLE
DOES THAT MEAN YOUR CUTE LITTLE FRIEND WOULD LIKE SOME MORE?
NAH. HUPPO, HE JUSTA HAS TO TINKLE!
END.

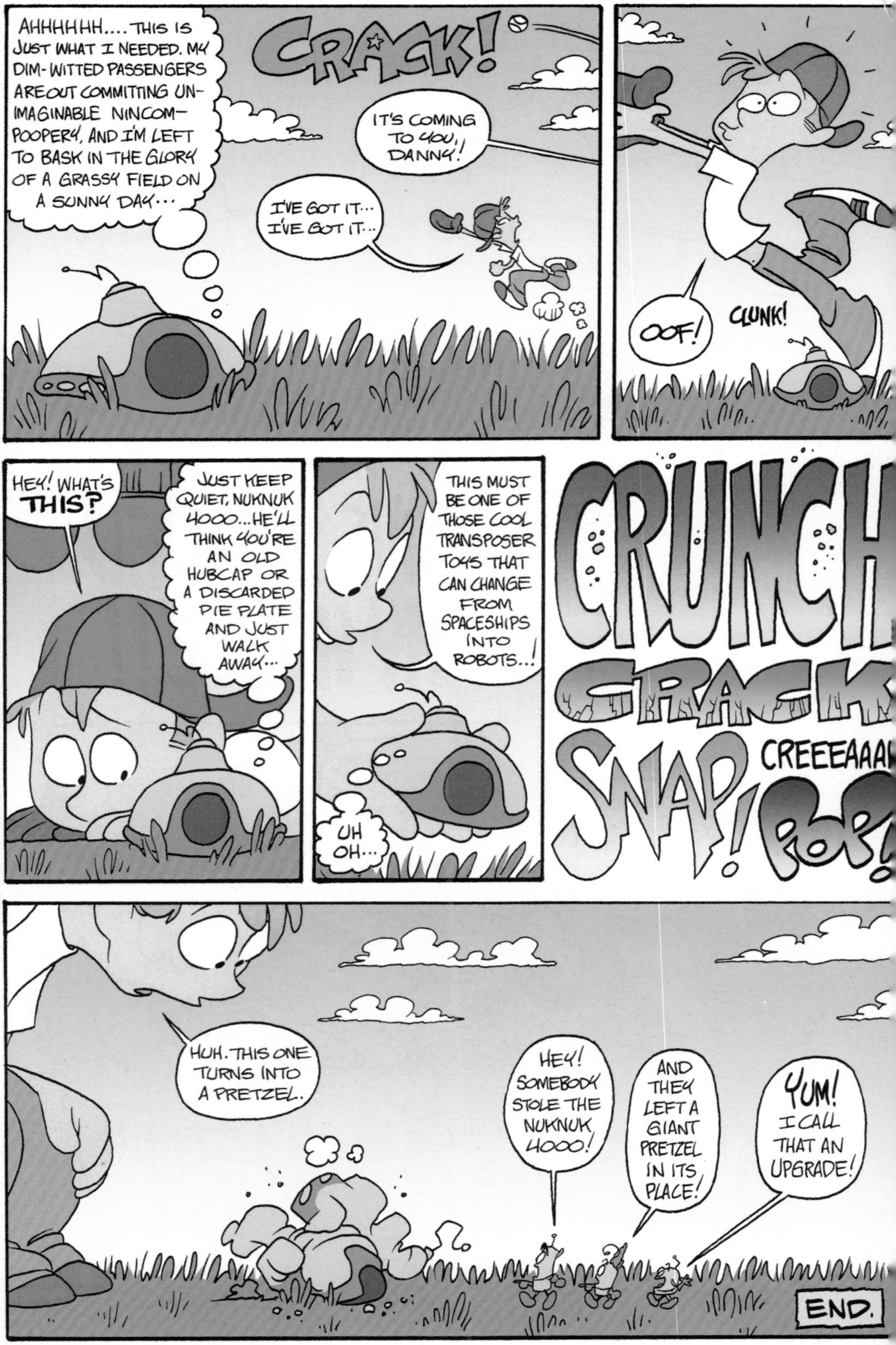
AHHHHHH.... THIS IS JUST WHAT I NEEDED. MY DIM-WITTED PASSENGERS ARE OUT COMMITTING UN-IMAGINABLE NINCOM-POOPERY, AND I'M LEFT TO BASK IN THE GLORY OF A GRASSY FIELD ON A SUNNY DAY...
CRACK!
IT'S COMING TO YOU, DANNY!
I'VE GOT IT... I'VE GOT IT...
OOF!
CLUNK!
HEY! WHAT'S THIS?
JUST KEEP QUIET, NUKNUK 4000... HE'LL THINK YOU'RE AN OLD HUBCAP OR A DISCARDED PIE PLATE AND JUST WALK AWAY...
THIS MUST BE ONE OF THOSE COOL TRANSPOSER TOYS THAT CAN CHANGE FROM SPACESHIPS INTO ROBOTS...!
UH OH...
CRUNCH
CRACK
SNAP!
CREEEAAA
POP!
HUH. THIS ONE TURNS INTO A PRETZEL.
HEY! SOMEBODY STOLE THE NUKNUK 4000!
AND THEY LEFT A GIANT PRETZEL IN ITS PLACE!
YUM! I CALL THAT AN UPGRADE!
END.

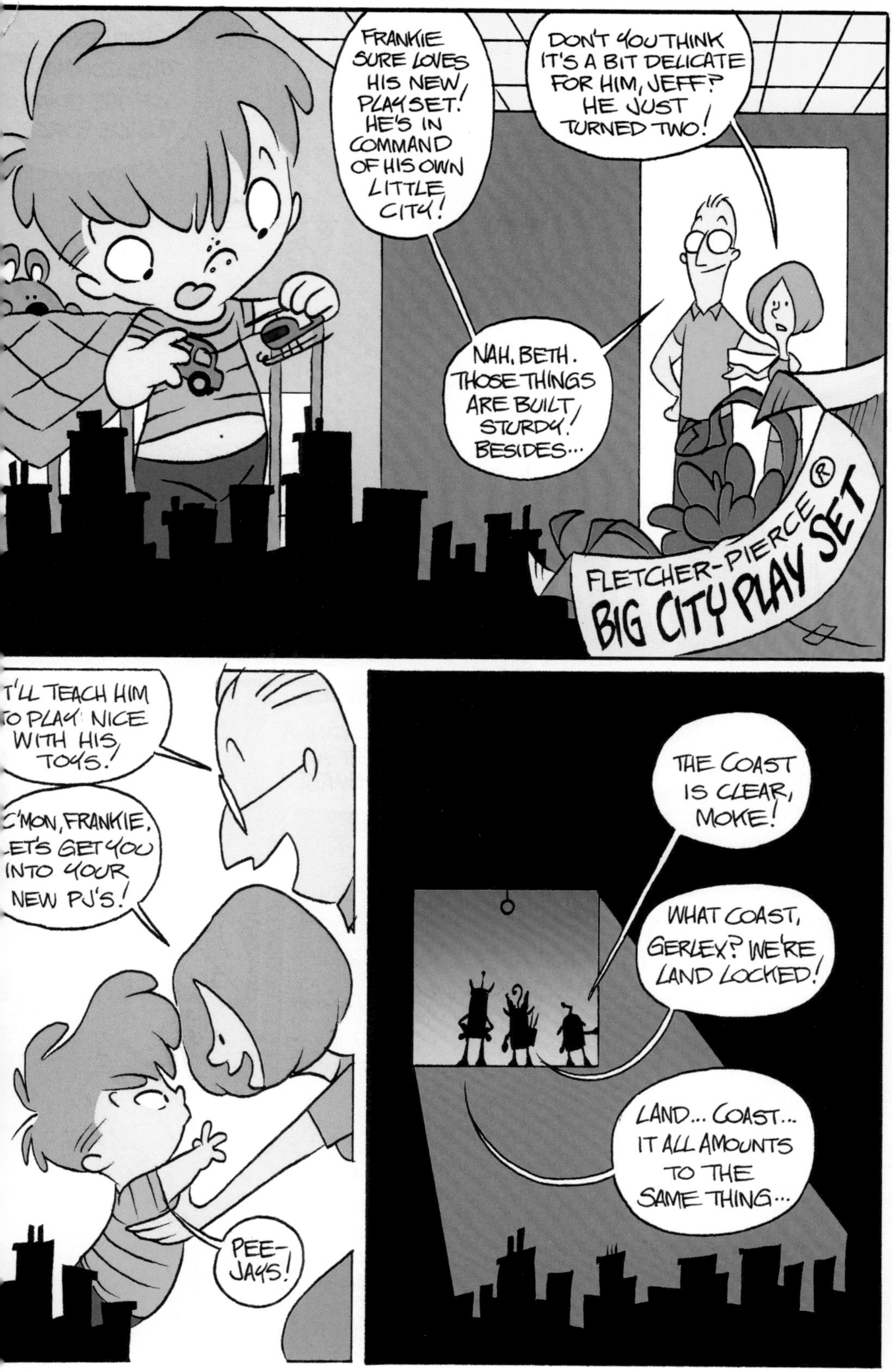
FRANKIE SURE LOVES HIS NEW PLAYSET! HE'S IN COMMAND OF HIS OWN LITTLE CITY!
DON'T YOU THINK IT'S A BIT DELICATE FOR HIM, JEFF? HE JUST TURNED TWO!
NAH, BETH. THOSE THINGS ARE BUILT STURDY! BESIDES...
FLETCHER-PIERCE® BIG CITY PLAY SET
T'LL TEACH HIM O PLAY NICE WITH HIS TOYS!
C'MON, FRANKIE, ET'S GET YOU INTO YOUR NEW PJ'S!
PEE-JAYS!
THE COAST IS CLEAR, MOKE!
WHAT COAST, GERLEX? WE'RE LAND LOCKED!
LAND... COAST... IT ALL AMOUNTS TO THE SAME THING...

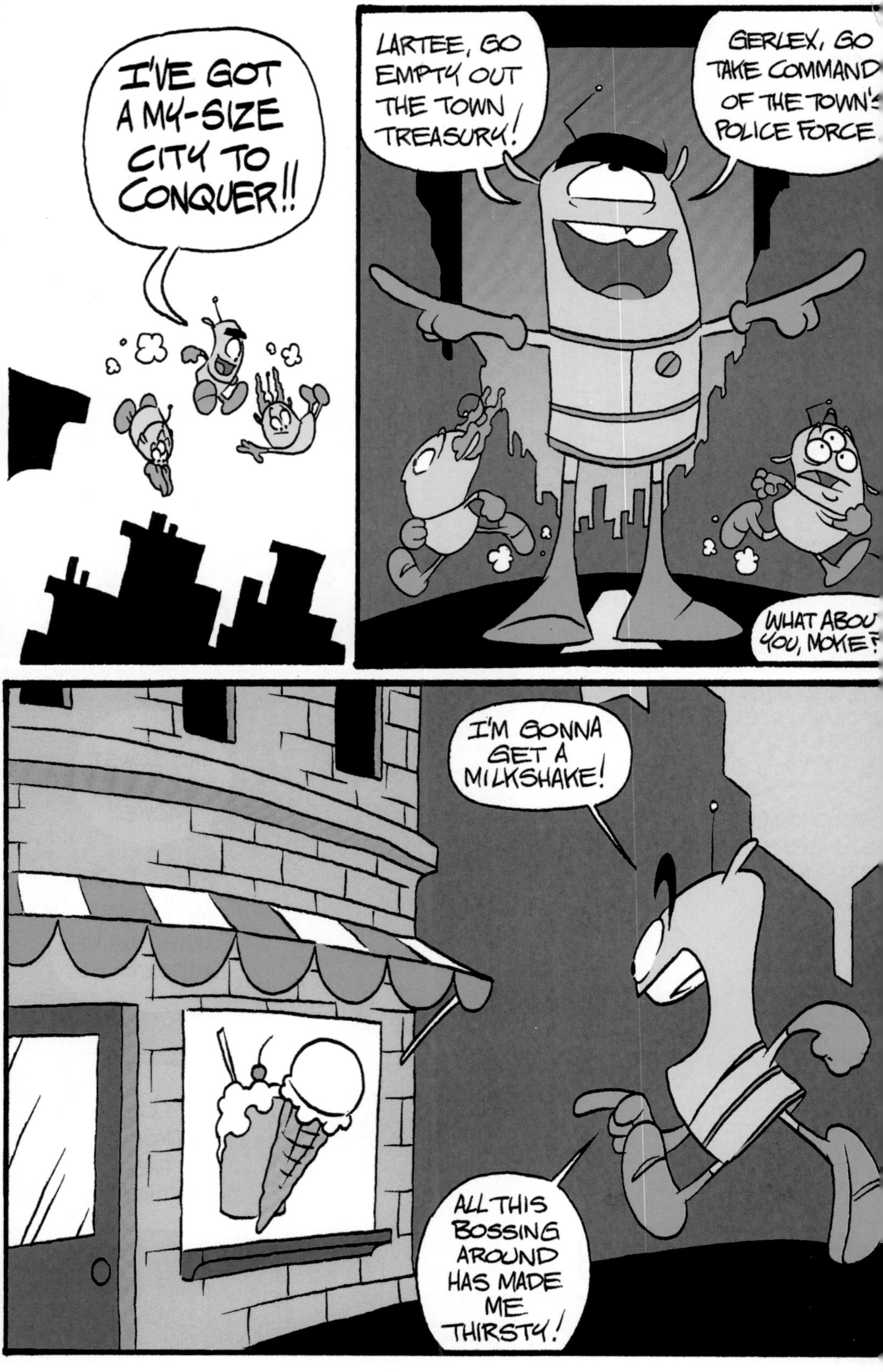
I'VE GOT A MY-SIZE CITY TO CONQUER!!
LARTEE, GO EMPTY OUT THE TOWN TREASURY!
GERLEX, GO TAKE COMMAND OF THE TOWN'S POLICE FORCE.
WHAT ABOU YOU, MOKE?
I'M GONNA GET A MILKSHAKE!
ALL THIS BOSSING AROUND HAS MADE ME THIRSTY!

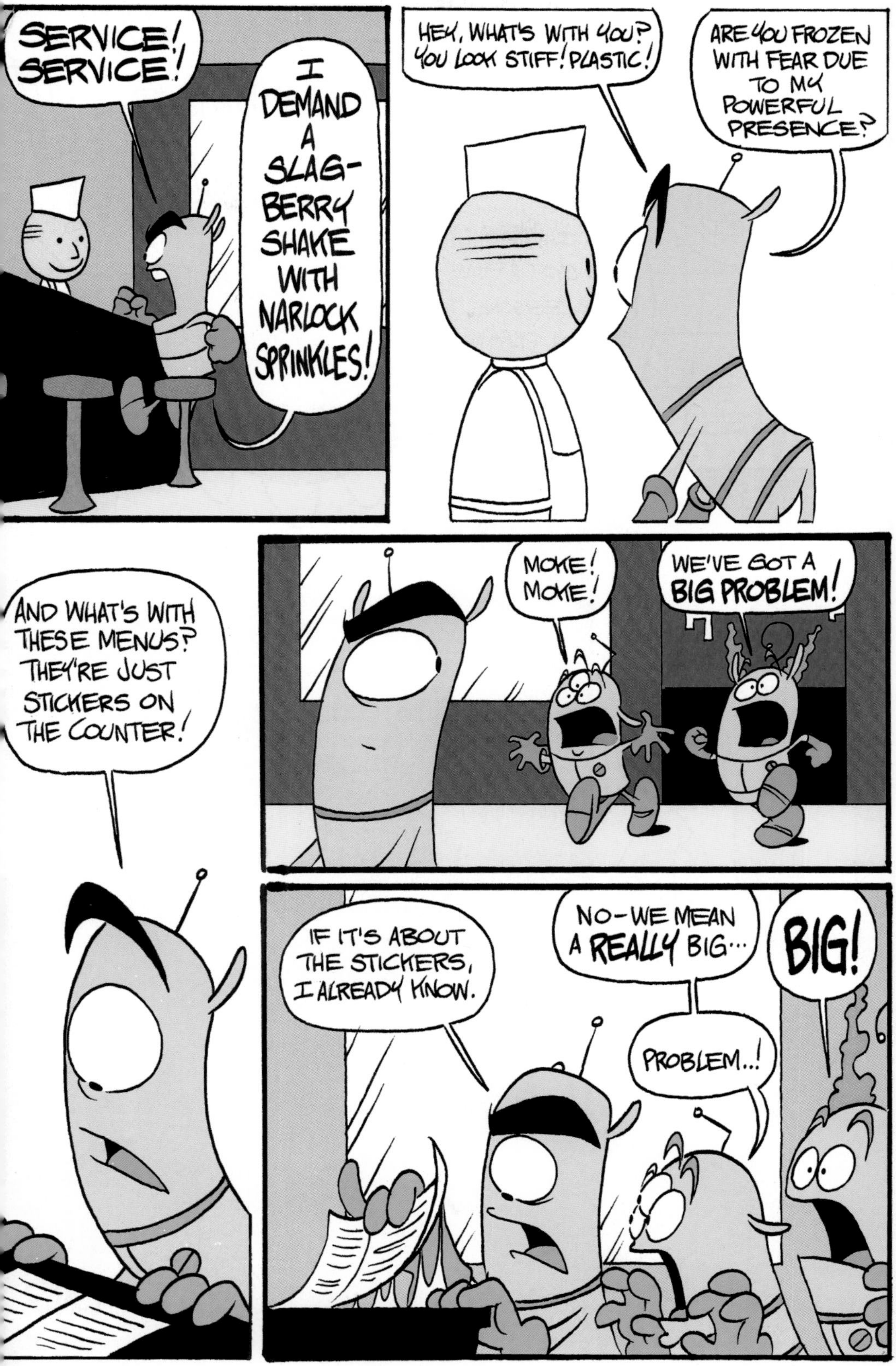
SERVICE! SERVICE!
I DEMAND A SLAG-BERRY SHAKE WITH NARLOCK SPRINKLES!
HEY, WHAT'S WITH YOU? YOU LOOK STIFF! PLASTIC!
ARE YOU FROZEN WITH FEAR DUE TO MY POWERFUL PRESENCE?
AND WHAT'S WITH THESE MENUS? THEY'RE JUST STICKERS ON THE COUNTER!
MOKE! MOKE!
WE'VE GOT A BIG PROBLEM!
IF IT'S ABOUT THE STICKERS, I ALREADY KNOW.
NO-WE MEAN A REALLY BIG...
PROBLEM...!
BIG!

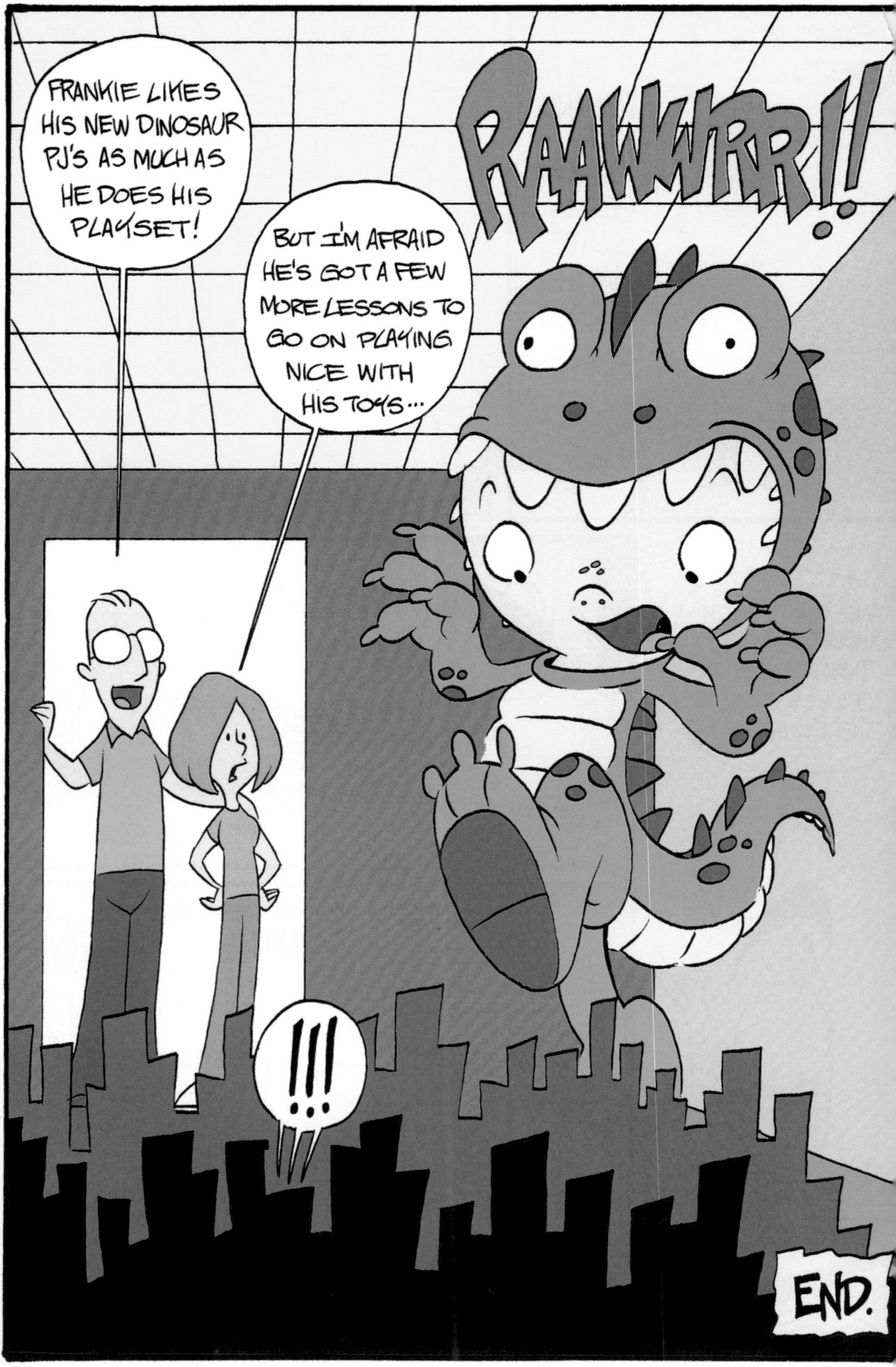
FRANKIE LIKES HIS NEW DINOSAUR PJ'S AS MUCH AS HE DOES HIS PLAYSET!
BUT I'M AFRAID HE'S GOT A FEW MORE LESSONS TO GO ON PLAYING NICE WITH HIS TOYS...
RAAWWRRR!!
!!!
END.

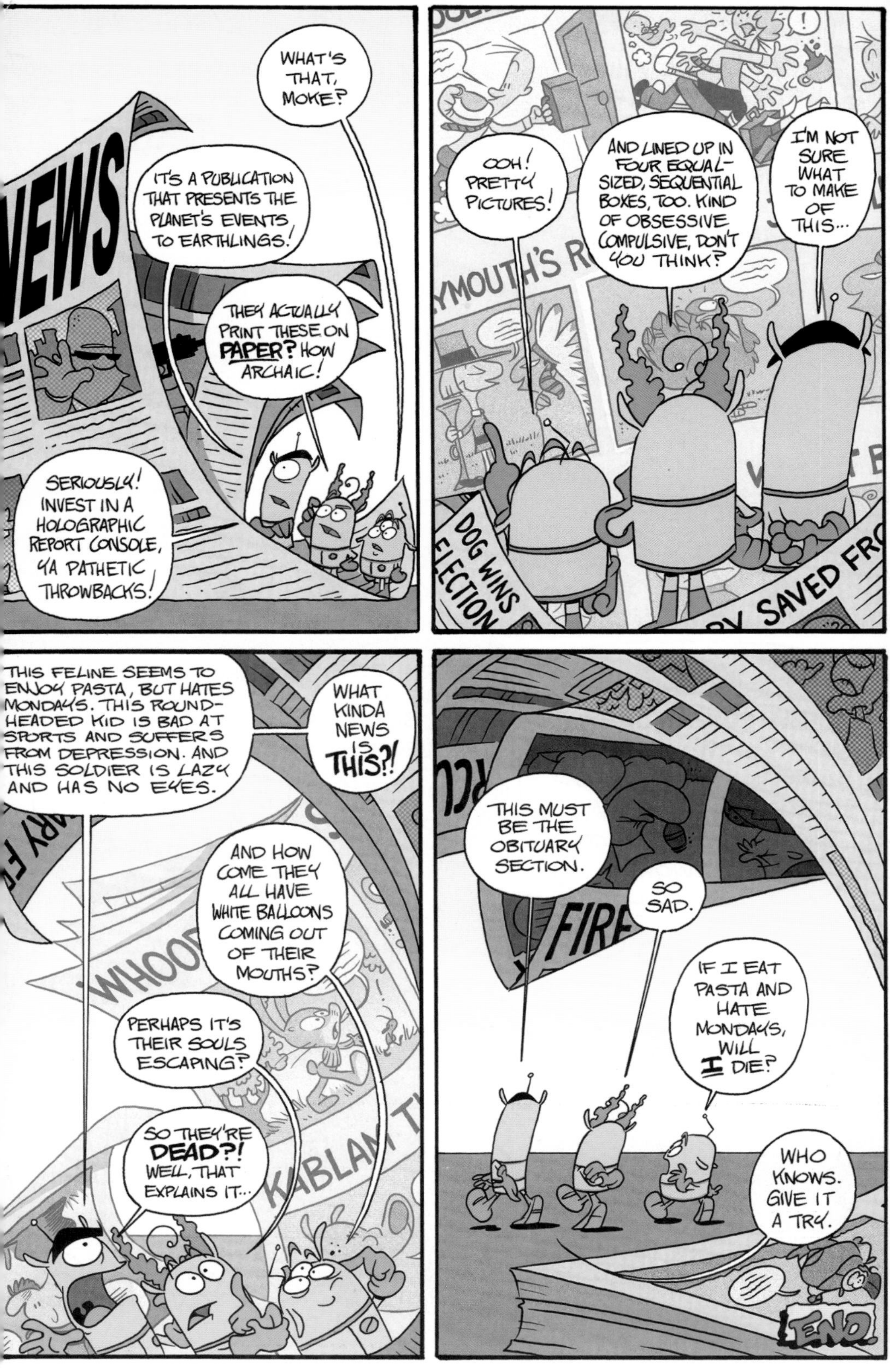
WHAT'S THAT, MOKE?
IT'S A PUBLICATION THAT PRESENTS THE PLANET'S EVENTS TO EARTHLINGS!
THEY ACTUALLY PRINT THESE ON PAPER? HOW ARCHAIC!
SERIOUSLY! INVEST IN A HOLOGRAPHIC REPORT CONSOLE, YA PATHETIC THROWBACKS!
NEWS
OOH! PRETTY PICTURES!
AND LINED UP IN FOUR EQUAL-SIZED, SEQUENTIAL BOXES, TOO. KIND OF OBSESSIVE COMPULSIVE, DON'T YOU THINK?
I'M NOT SURE WHAT TO MAKE OF THIS...
DOG WINS ELECTION
SAVED FRO
THIS FELINE SEEMS TO ENJOY PASTA, BUT HATES MONDAYS. THIS ROUND-HEADED KID IS BAD AT SPORTS AND SUFFERS FROM DEPRESSION. AND THIS SOLDIER IS LAZY AND HAS NO EYES.
WHAT KINDA NEWS IS THIS?!
AND HOW COME THEY ALL HAVE WHITE BALLOONS COMING OUT OF THEIR MOUTHS?
PERHAPS IT'S THEIR SOULS ESCAPING?
SO THEY'RE DEAD?! WELL, THAT EXPLAINS IT...
WHOOD
KABLAM
THIS MUST BE THE OBITUARY SECTION.
SO SAD.
FIRE
IF I EAT PASTA AND HATE MONDAYS, WILL I DIE?
WHO KNOWS. GIVE IT A TRY.
END

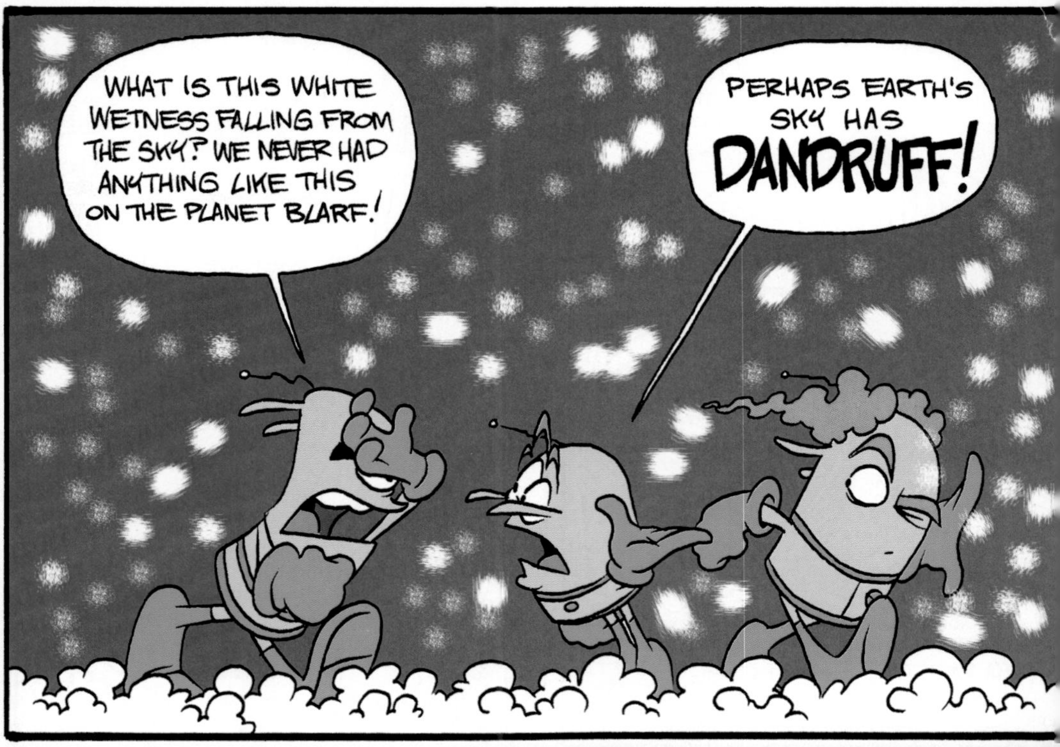
WHAT IS THIS WHITE WETNESS FALLING FROM THE SKY? WE NEVER HAD ANYTHING LIKE THIS ON THE PLANET BLARF!
PERHAPS EARTH'S SKY HAS DANDRUFF!
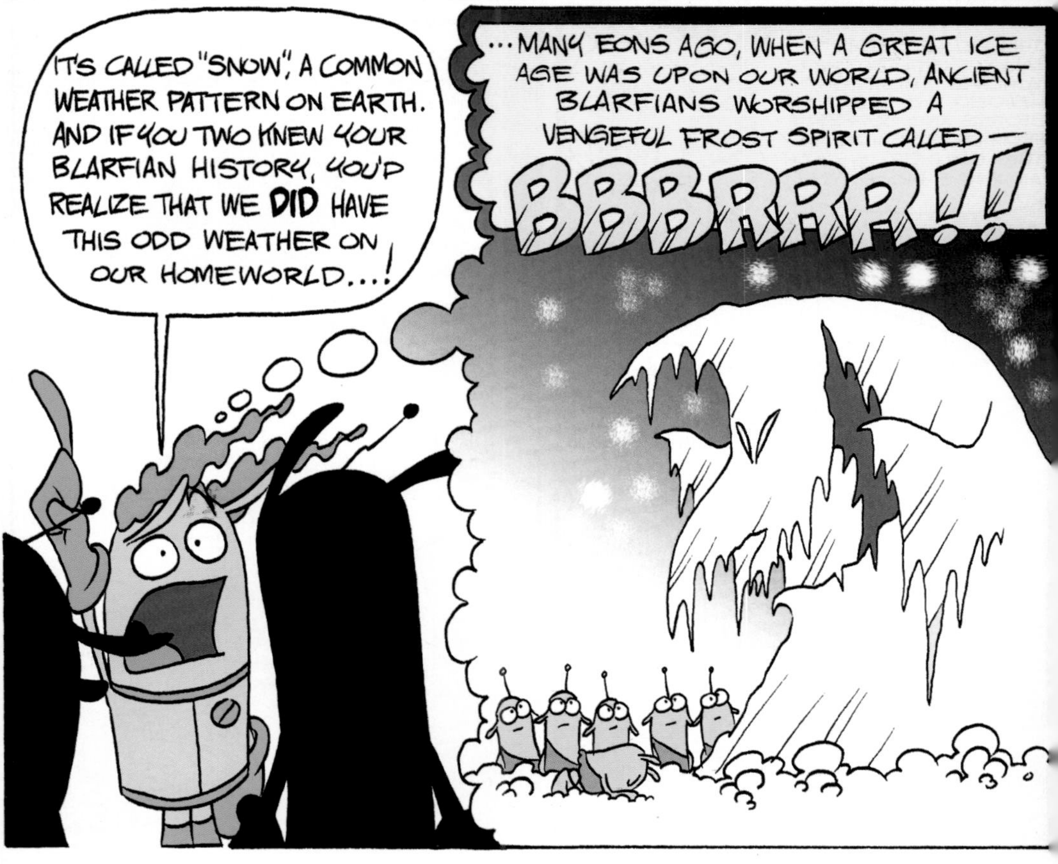
IT'S CALLED "SNOW", A COMMON WEATHER PATTERN ON EARTH. AND IF YOU TWO KNEW YOUR BLARFIAN HISTORY, YOU'D REALIZE THAT WE DID HAVE THIS ODD WEATHER ON OUR HOMEWORLD...!
...MANY EONS AGO, WHEN A GREAT ICE AGE WAS UPON OUR WORLD, ANCIENT BLARFIANS WORSHIPPED A VENGEFUL FROST SPIRIT CALLED—
BBBRRR!!

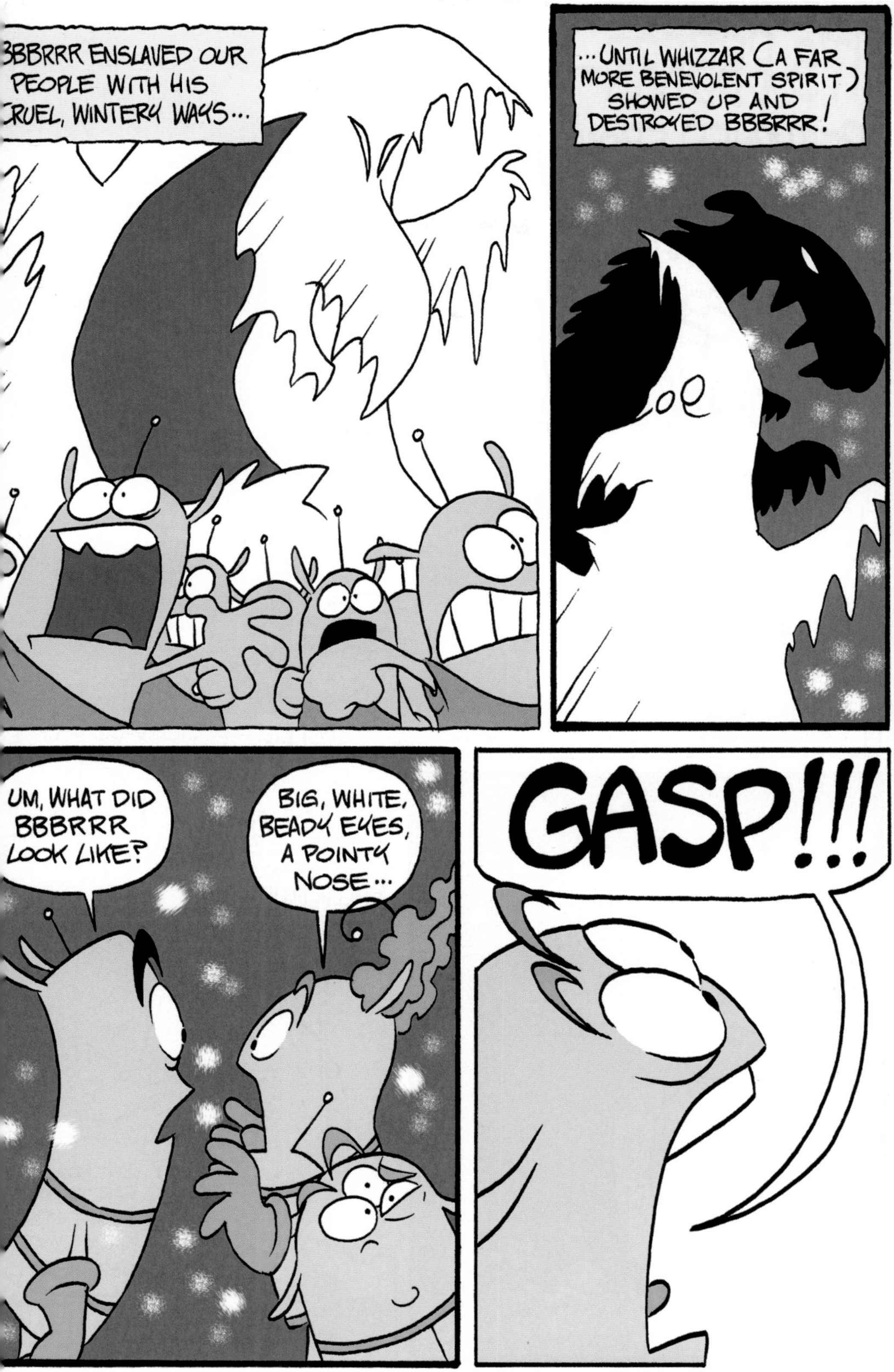
BBBRRR ENSLAVED OUR PEOPLE WITH HIS CRUEL, WINTERY WAYS...
...UNTIL WHIZZAR (A FAR MORE BENEVOLENT SPIRIT) SHOWED UP AND DESTROYED BBBRRR!
UM, WHAT DID BBBRRR LOOK LIKE?
BIG, WHITE, BEADY EYES, A POINTY NOSE...
GASP!!!

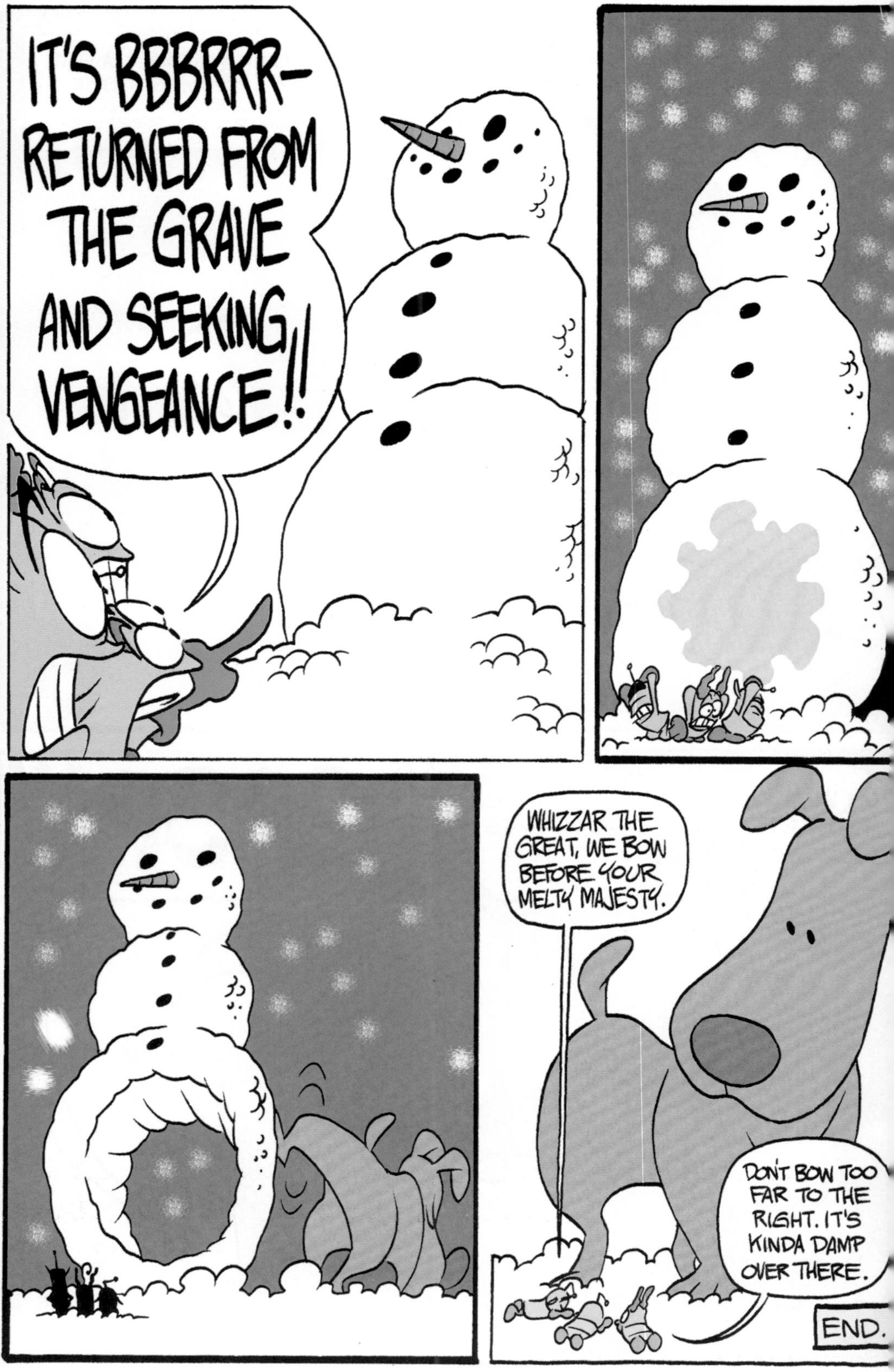
IT'S BBBRRR-RETURNED FROM THE GRAVE AND SEEKING VENGEANCE!!
WHIZZAR THE GREAT, WE BOW BEFORE YOUR MELTY MAJESTY.
DON'T BOW TOO FAR TO THE RIGHT. IT'S KINDA DAMP OVER THERE.
END.

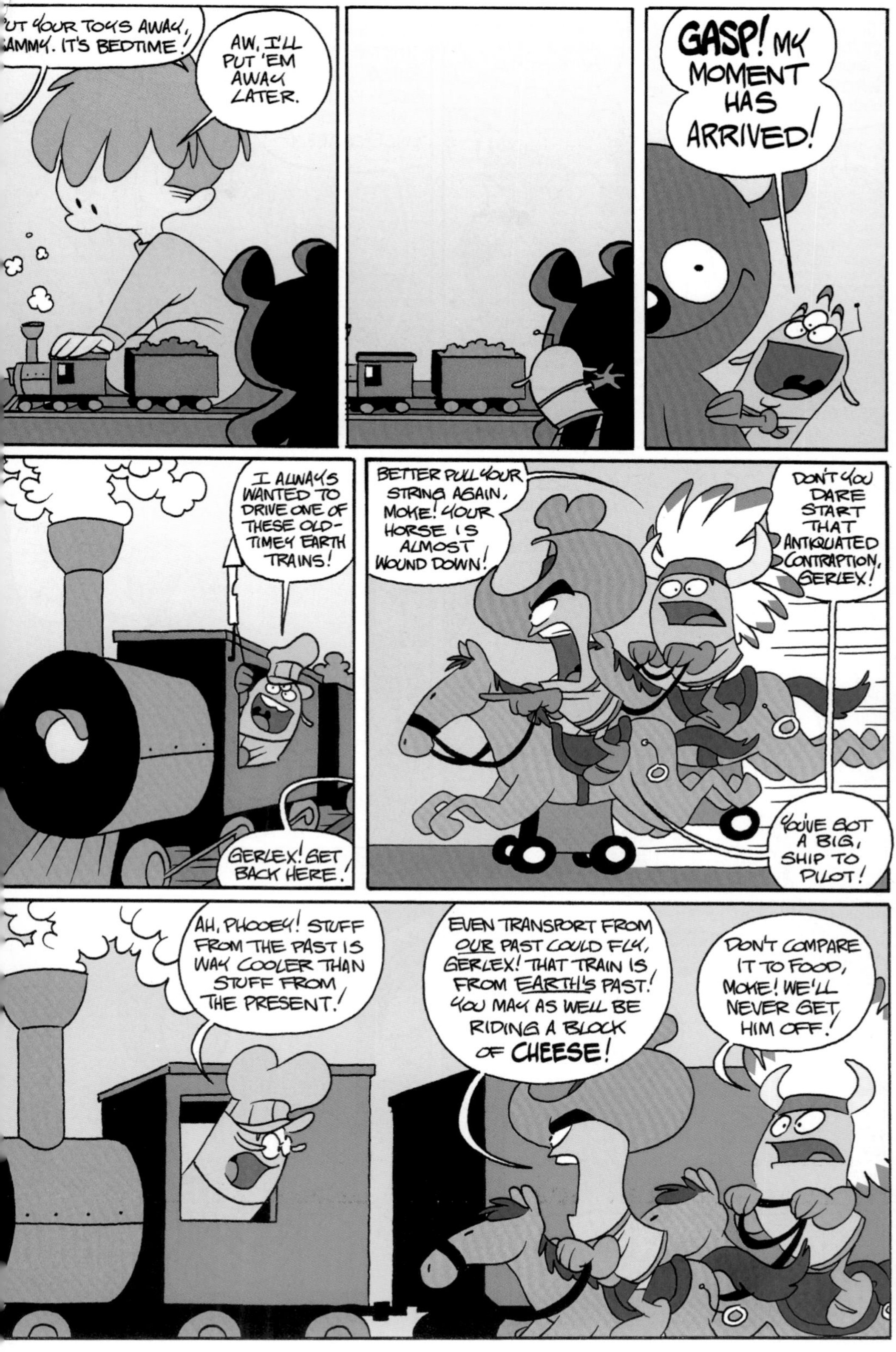
PUT YOUR TOYS AWAY, SAMMY. IT'S BEDTIME!
AW, I'LL PUT 'EM AWAY LATER.
GASP! MY MOMENT HAS ARRIVED!
I ALWAYS WANTED TO DRIVE ONE OF THESE OLD-TIMEY EARTH TRAINS!
GERLEX! GET BACK HERE!
BETTER PULL YOUR STRING AGAIN, MOKE! YOUR HORSE IS ALMOST WOUND DOWN!
DON'T YOU DARE START THAT ANTIQUATED CONTRAPTION, GERLEX!
YOU'VE GOT A BIG, SHIP TO PILOT!
AH, PHOOEY! STUFF FROM THE PAST IS WAY COOLER THAN STUFF FROM THE PRESENT!
EVEN TRANSPORT FROM OUR PAST COULD FLY, GERLEX! THAT TRAIN IS FROM EARTH'S PAST! YOU MAY AS WELL BE RIDING A BLOCK OF CHEESE!
DON'T COMPARE IT TO FOOD, MOKE! WE'LL NEVER GET HIM OFF!

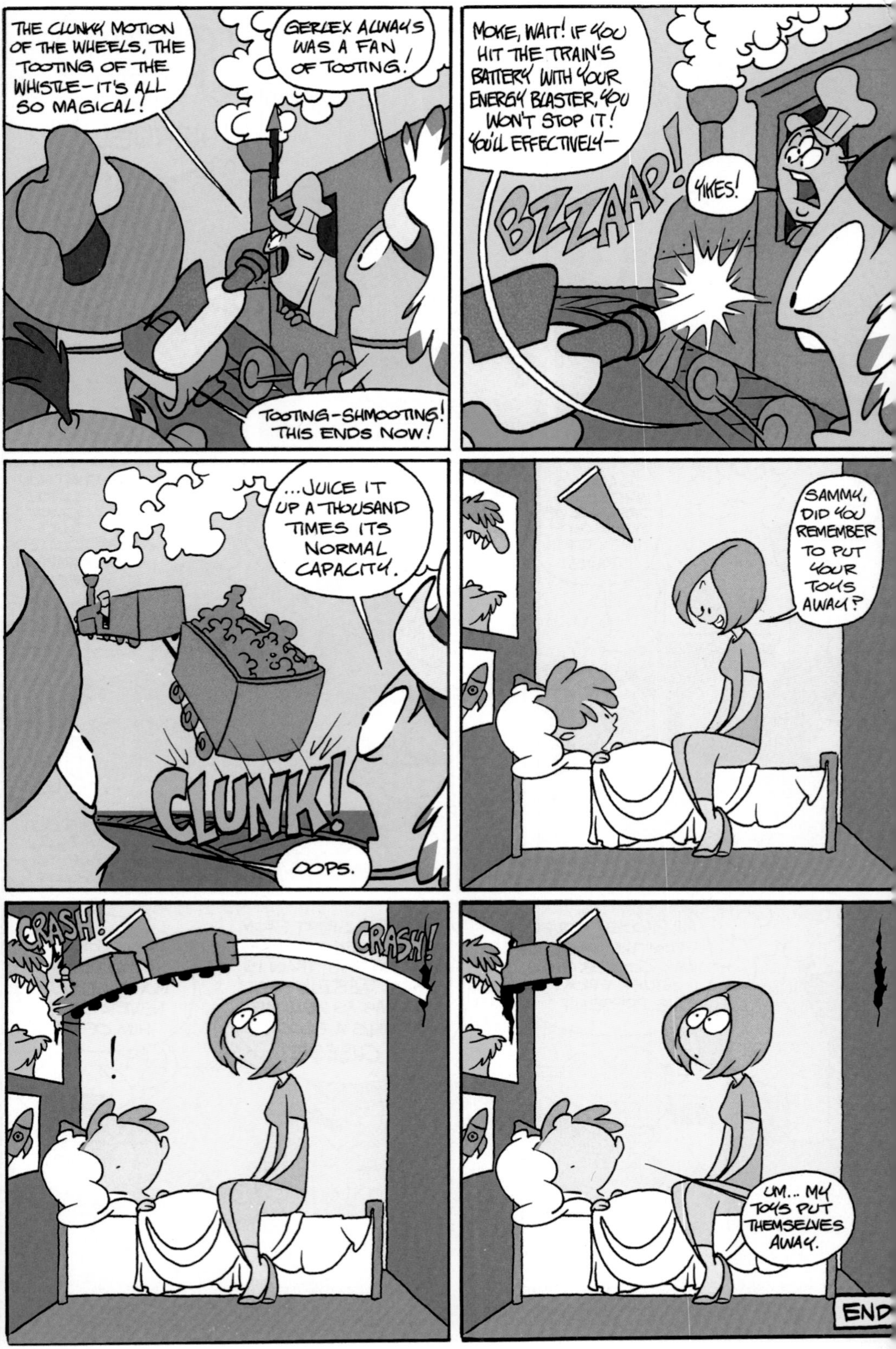
THE CLUNKY MOTION OF THE WHEELS, THE TOOTING OF THE WHISTLE—IT'S ALL SO MAGICAL!
GERLEX ALWAYS WAS A FAN OF TOOTING!
TOOTING-SHMOOTING! THIS ENDS NOW!
MOKE, WAIT! IF YOU HIT THE TRAIN'S BATTERY WITH YOUR ENERGY BLASTER, YOU WON'T STOP IT! YOU'LL EFFECTIVELY—
BZZAAP!
YIKES!
...JUICE IT UP A THOUSAND TIMES ITS NORMAL CAPACITY.
CLUNK!
OOPS.
SAMMY, DID YOU REMEMBER TO PUT YOUR TOYS AWAY?
CRASH!
CRASH!
!
UM... MY TOYS PUT THEMSELVES AWAY.
END

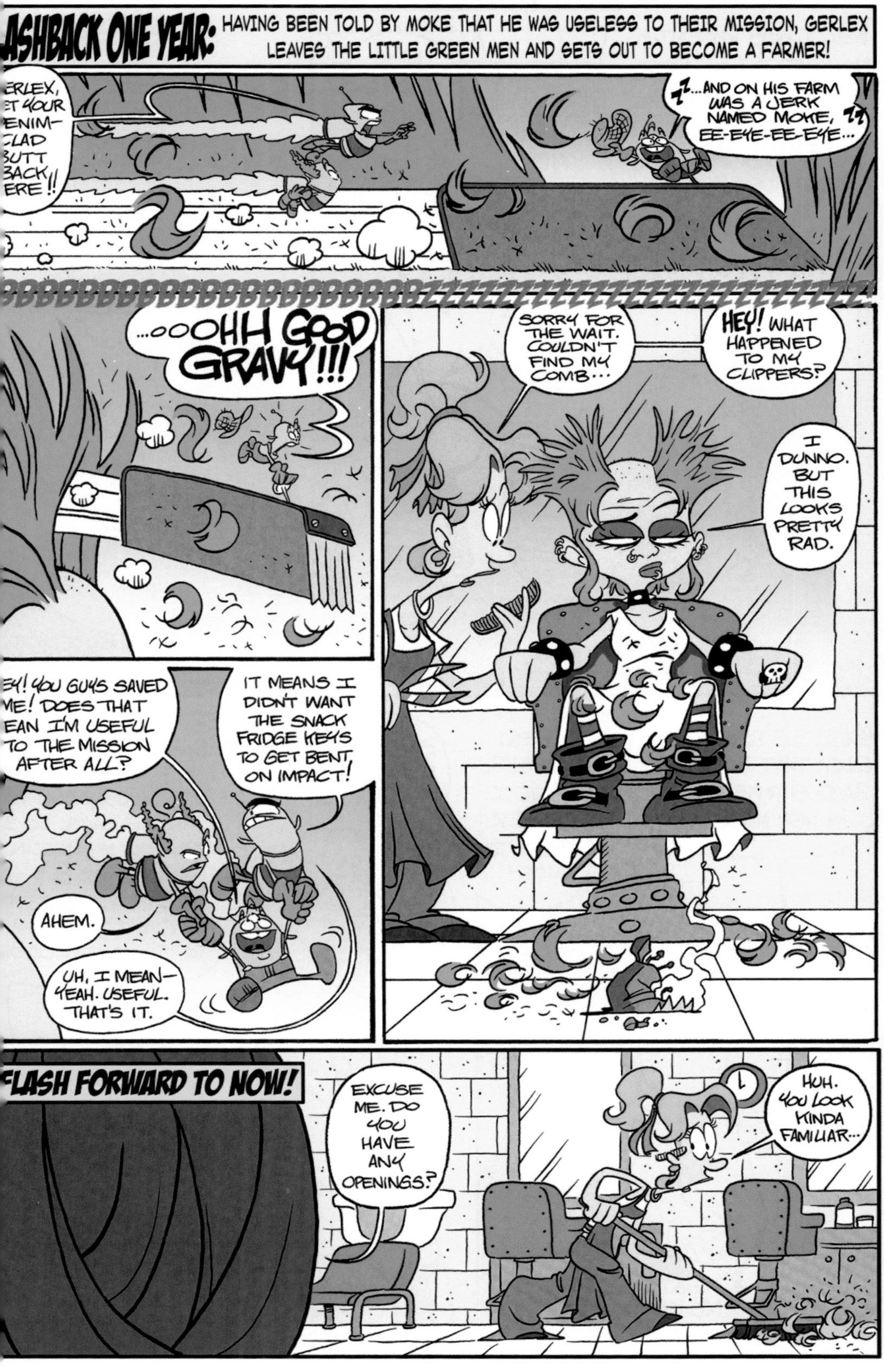

ASHBACK ONE YEAR:
HAVING BEEN TOLD BY MOKE THAT HE WAS USELESS TO THEIR MISSION, GERLEX LEAVES THE LITTLE GREEN MEN AND SETS OUT TO BECOME A FARMER!
ERLEX, ET YOUR ENIM-CLAD BUTT BACK ERE!!
Z...AND ON HIS FARM WAS A JERK NAMED MOKE, EE-EYE-EE-EYE... ZZ
BBBBBBBBBBBBBBBBBBBBBBBBBZZZZZZZZZZZZZZZZZZZZZZZZZZZZZZZ!
...oooHH GOOD GRAVY!!!
SORRY FOR THE WAIT. COULDN'T FIND MY COMB...
HEY! WHAT HAPPENED TO MY CLIPPERS?
I DUNNO. BUT THIS LOOKS PRETTY RAD.
EY! YOU GUYS SAVED ME! DOES THAT EAN I'M USEFUL TO THE MISSION AFTER ALL?
IT MEANS I DIDN'T WANT THE SNACK FRIDGE KEYS TO GET BENT ON IMPACT!
AHEM.
UH, I MEAN-YEAH. USEFUL. THAT'S IT.
FLASH FORWARD TO NOW!
EXCUSE ME. DO YOU HAVE ANY OPENINGS?
HUH. YOU LOOK KINDA FAMILIAR...

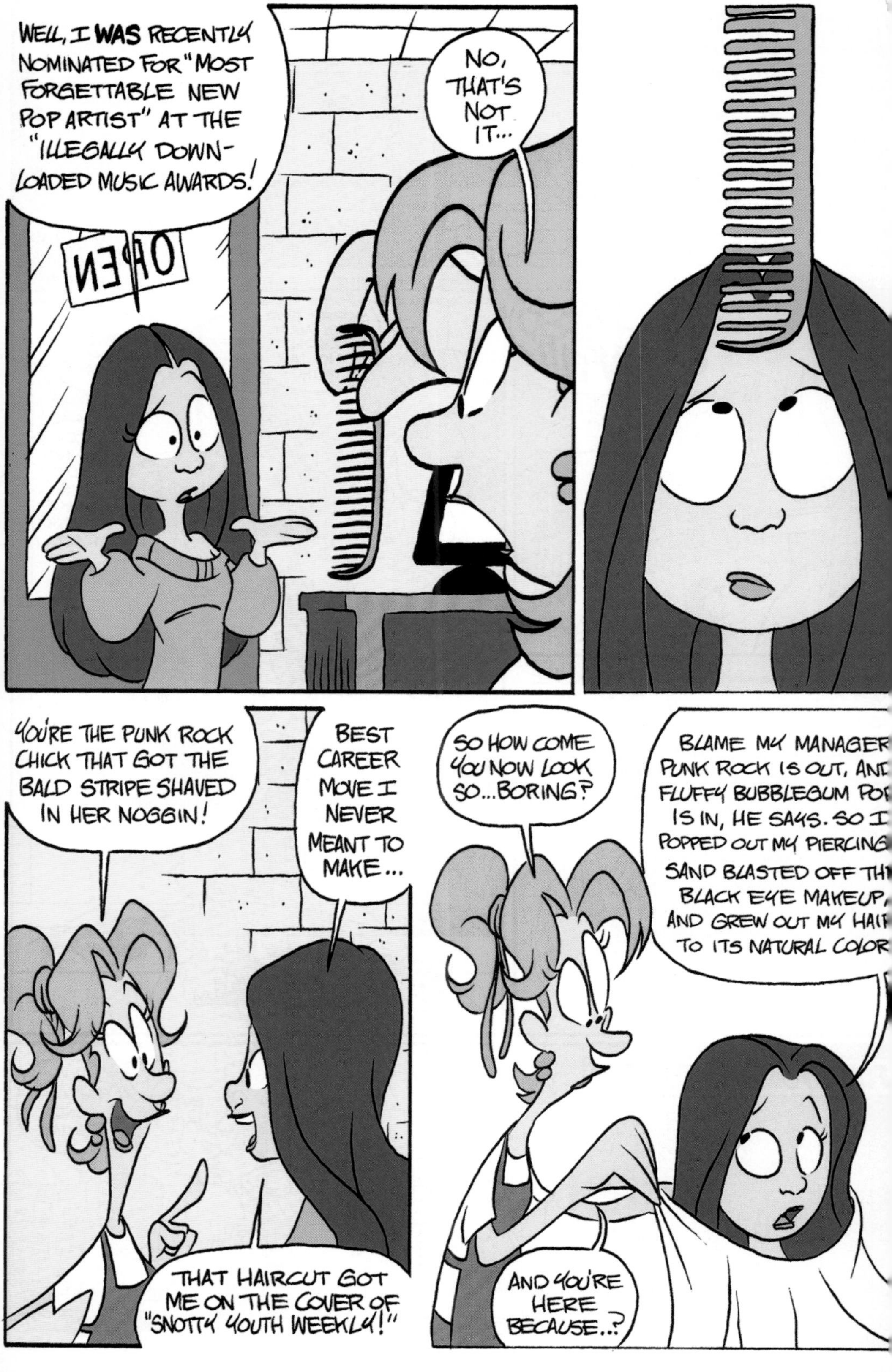
WELL, I **WAS** RECENTLY NOMINATED FOR "MOST FORGETTABLE NEW POP ARTIST" AT THE "ILLEGALLY DOWN-LOADED MUSIC AWARDS!
OPEN
NO, THAT'S NOT IT...
YOU'RE THE PUNK ROCK CHICK THAT GOT THE BALD STRIPE SHAVED IN HER NOGGIN!
BEST CAREER MOVE I NEVER MEANT TO MAKE...
THAT HAIRCUT GOT ME ON THE COVER OF "SNOTTY YOUTH WEEKLY!"
SO HOW COME YOU NOW LOOK SO...BORING?
BLAME MY MANAGER PUNK ROCK IS OUT, AND FLUFFY BUBBLEGUM POP IS IN, HE SAYS. SO I POPPED OUT MY PIERCINGS SAND BLASTED OFF THE BLACK EYE MAKEUP, AND GREW OUT MY HAIR TO ITS NATURAL COLOR
AND YOU'RE HERE BECAUSE..?

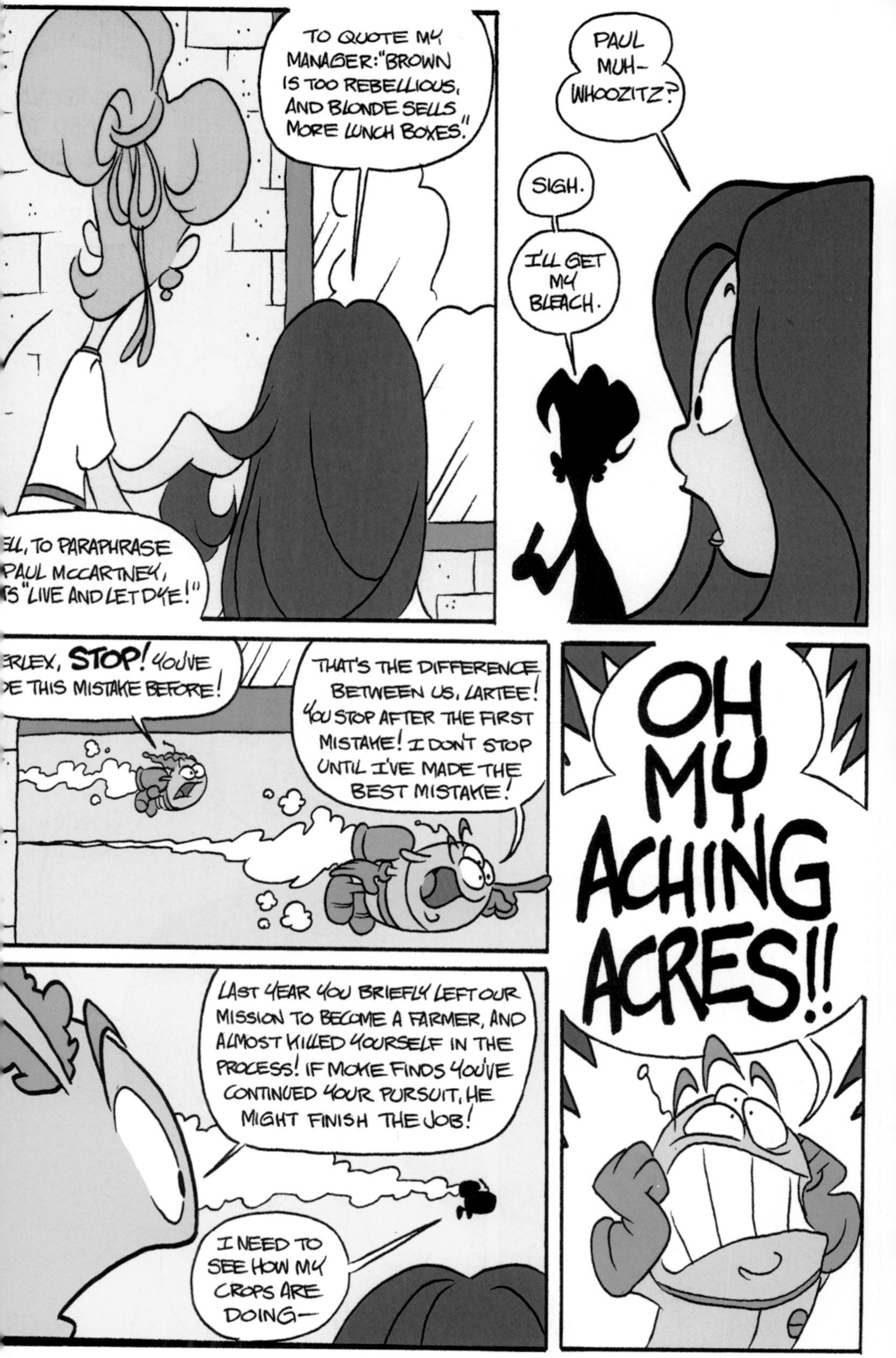
TO QUOTE MY MANAGER: "BROWN IS TOO REBELLIOUS, AND BLONDE SELLS MORE LUNCH BOXES."
ELL, TO PARAPHRASE PAUL McCARTNEY, TS "LIVE AND LET DYE!"
PAUL MUH-WHOOZITZ?
SIGH.
I'LL GET MY BLEACH.
ERLEX, STOP! YOU'VE DE THIS MISTAKE BEFORE!
THAT'S THE DIFFERENCE BETWEEN US, LARTEE! YOU STOP AFTER THE FIRST MISTAKE! I DON'T STOP UNTIL I'VE MADE THE BEST MISTAKE!
OH MY ACHING ACRES!!
LAST YEAR YOU BRIEFLY LEFT OUR MISSION TO BECOME A FARMER, AND ALMOST KILLED YOURSELF IN THE PROCESS! IF MOKE FINDS YOU'VE CONTINUED YOUR PURSUIT, HE MIGHT FINISH THE JOB!
I NEED TO SEE HOW MY CROPS ARE DOING—

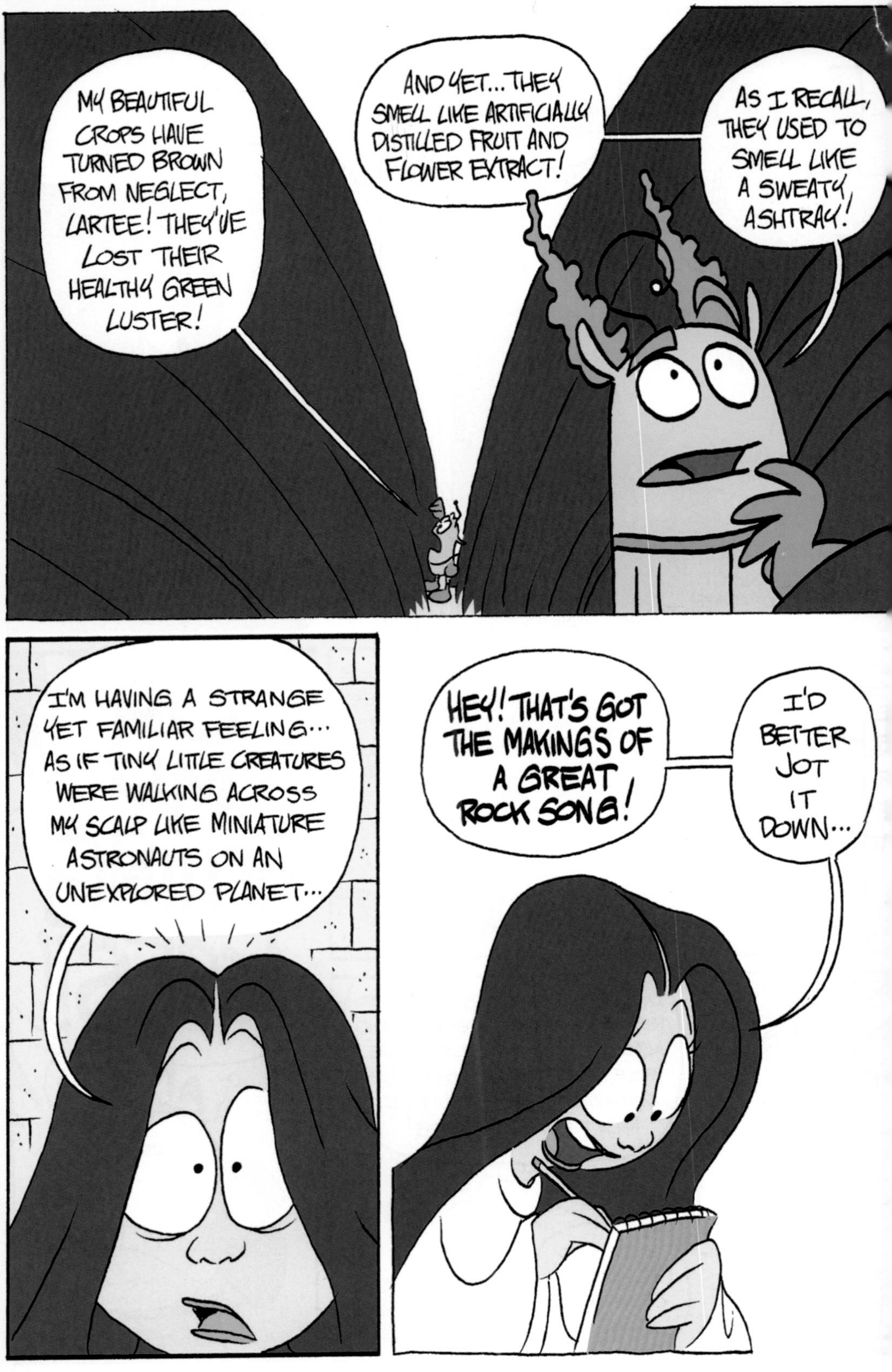
MY BEAUTIFUL CROPS HAVE TURNED BROWN FROM NEGLECT, LARTEE! THEY'VE LOST THEIR HEALTHY GREEN LUSTER!
AND YET... THEY SMELL LIKE ARTIFICIALLY DISTILLED FRUIT AND FLOWER EXTRACT!
AS I RECALL, THEY USED TO SMELL LIKE A SWEATY, ASHTRAY!
I'M HAVING A STRANGE YET FAMILIAR FEELING... AS IF TINY LITTLE CREATURES WERE WALKING ACROSS MY SCALP LIKE MINIATURE ASTRONAUTS ON AN UNEXPLORED PLANET...
HEY! THAT'S GOT THE MAKINGS OF A GREAT ROCK SONG!
I'D BETTER JOT IT DOWN...

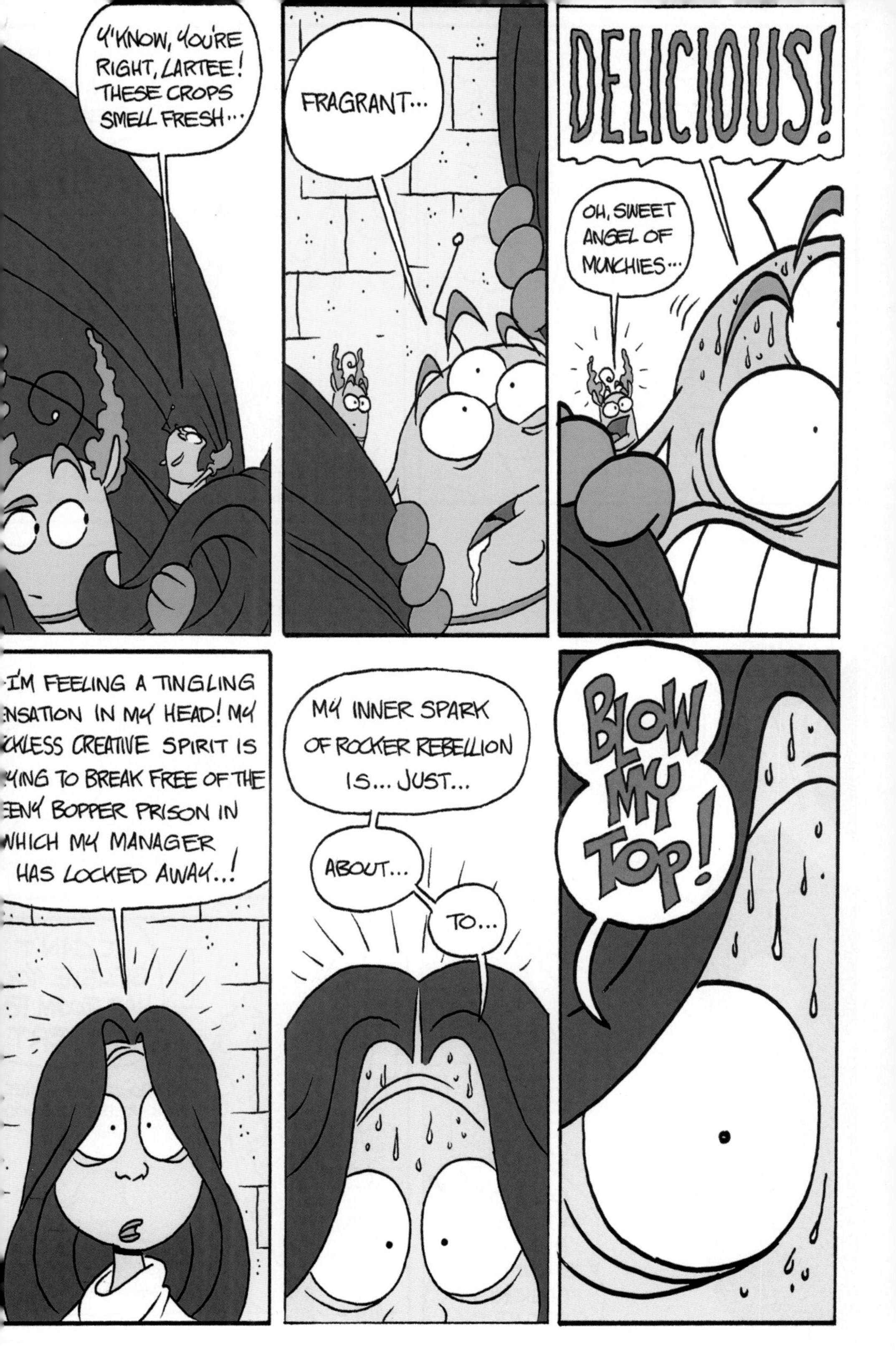

Y'KNOW, YOU'RE RIGHT, LARTEE! THESE CROPS SMELL FRESH...
FRAGRANT...
DELICIOUS!
OH, SWEET ANGEL OF MUNCHIES...
I'M FEELING A TINGLING NSATION IN MY HEAD! MY CKLESS CREATIVE SPIRIT IS YING TO BREAK FREE OF THE EENY BOPPER PRISON IN WHICH MY MANAGER HAS LOCKED AWAY...!
MY INNER SPARK OF ROCKER REBELLION IS... JUST...
ABOUT...
TO...
BLOW MY TOP!

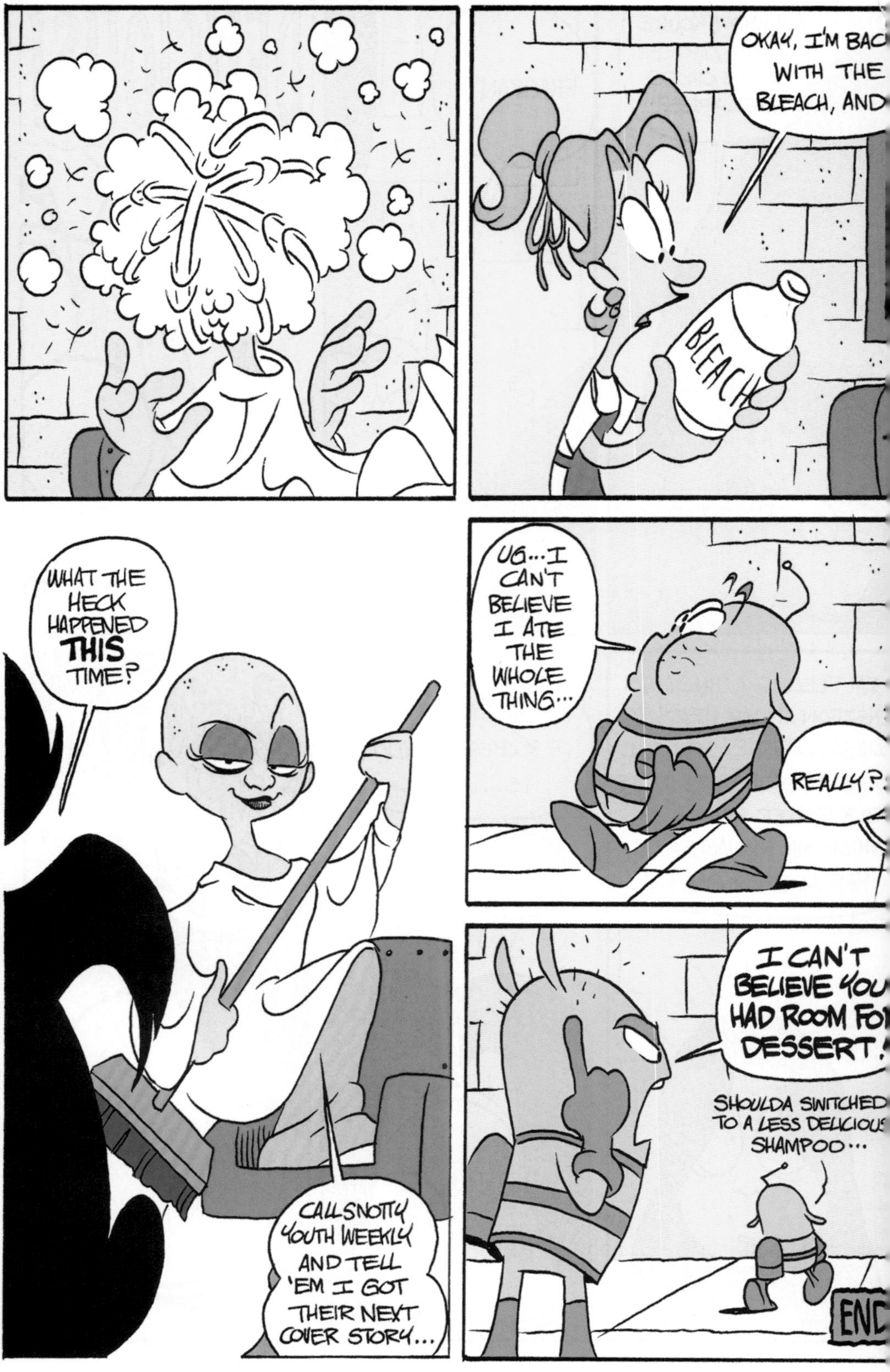
OKAY, I'M BAC
WITH THE
BLEACH, AND
BLEACH
WHAT THE HECK HAPPENED THIS TIME?
CALL SNOTTY YOUTH WEEKLY AND TELL 'EM I GOT THEIR NEXT COVER STORY...
UG... I CAN'T BELIEVE I ATE THE WHOLE THING...
REALLY?
I CAN'T BELIEVE YOU HAD ROOM FO DESSERT!
SHOULDA SWITCHED TO A LESS DELICIOUS SHAMPOO...
END

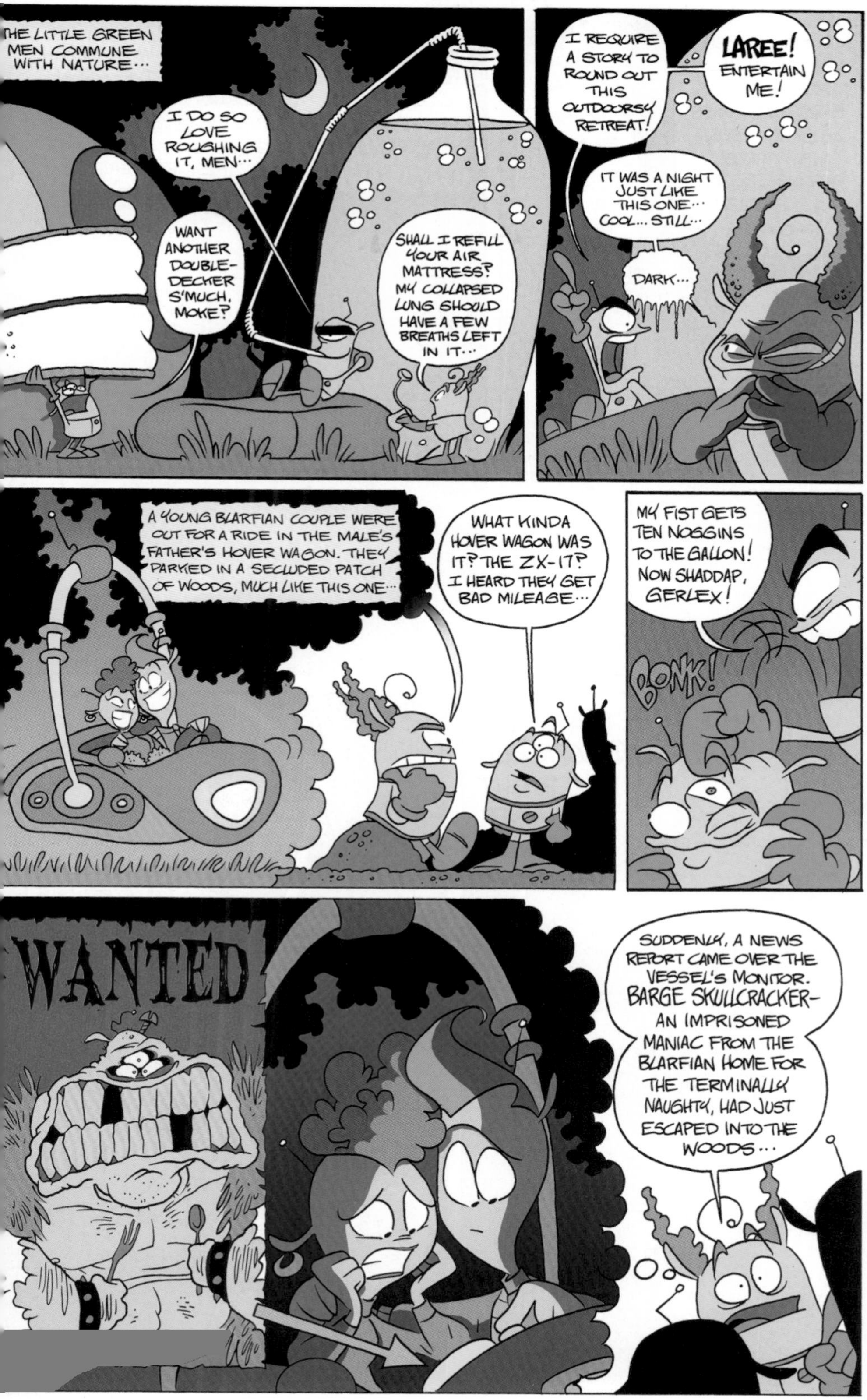
THE LITTLE GREEN MEN COMMUNE WITH NATURE...
I DO SO LOVE ROUGHING IT, MEN...
WANT ANOTHER DOUBLE-DECKER S'MUCH, MOKE?
SHALL I REFILL YOUR AIR MATTRESS? MY COLLAPSED LUNG SHOULD HAVE A FEW BREATHS LEFT IN IT...
I REQUIRE A STORY TO ROUND OUT THIS OUTDOORSY RETREAT!
LAREE! ENTERTAIN ME!
IT WAS A NIGHT JUST LIKE THIS ONE... COOL... STILL...
DARK...
A YOUNG BLARFIAN COUPLE WERE OUT FOR A RIDE IN THE MALE'S FATHER'S HOVER WAGON. THEY PARKED IN A SECLUDED PATCH OF WOODS, MUCH LIKE THIS ONE...
WHAT KINDA HOVER WAGON WAS IT? THE ZX-17? I HEARD THEY GET BAD MILEAGE...
MY FIST GETS TEN NOGGINS TO THE GALLON! NOW SHADDAP, GERLEX!
BONK!
WANTED
SUDDENLY, A NEWS REPORT CAME OVER THE VESSEL'S MONITOR. BARGE SKULLCRACKER- AN IMPRISONED MANIAC FROM THE BLARFIAN HOME FOR THE TERMINALLY NAUGHTY, HAD JUST ESCAPED INTO THE WOODS...

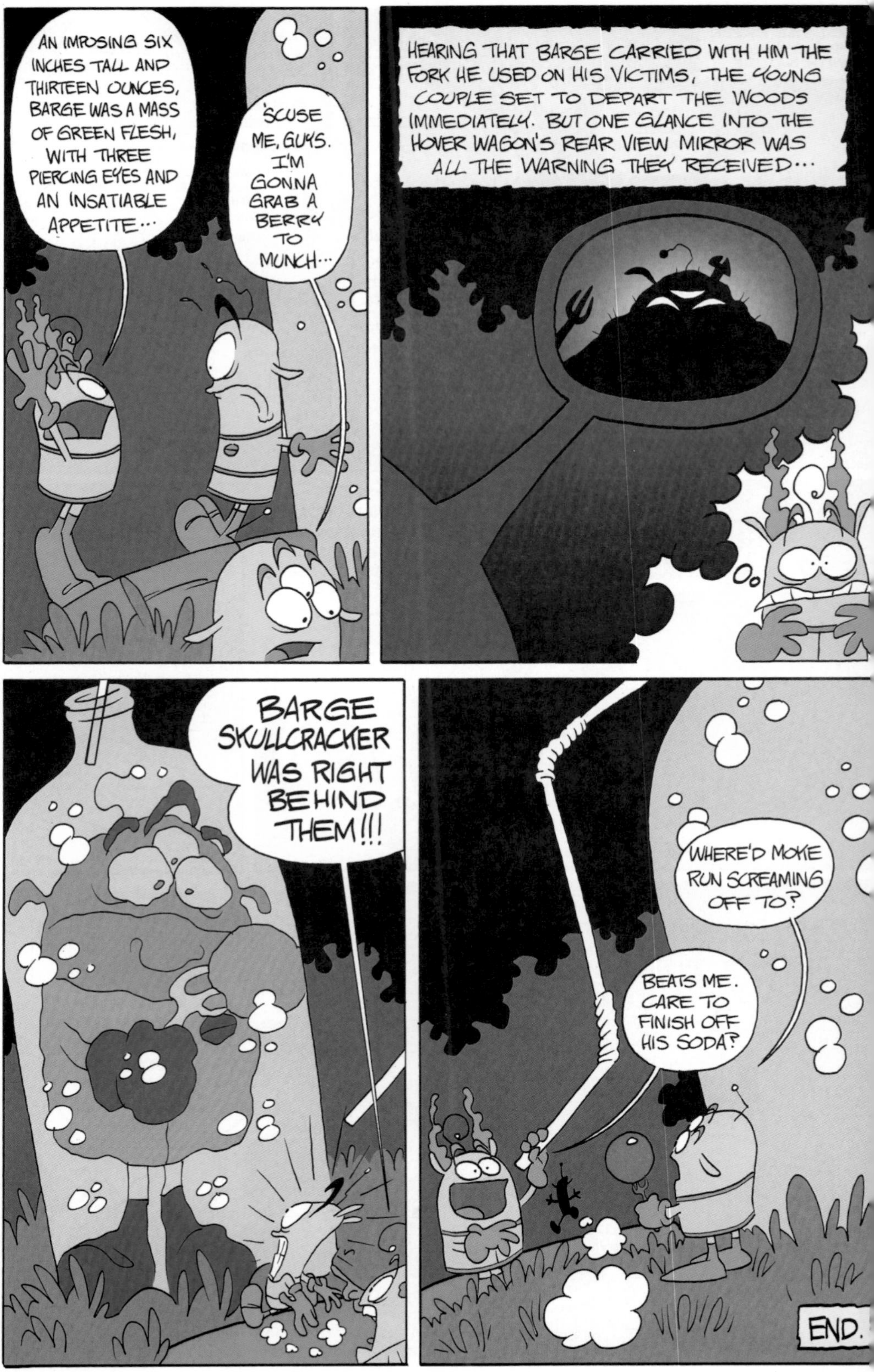
AN IMPOSING SIX INCHES TALL AND THIRTEEN OUNCES, BARGE WAS A MASS OF GREEN FLESH, WITH THREE PIERCING EYES AND AN INSATIABLE APPETITE...
'SCUSE ME, GUYS. I'M GONNA GRAB A BERRY TO MUNCH...
HEARING THAT BARGE CARRIED WITH HIM THE FORK HE USED ON HIS VICTIMS, THE YOUNG COUPLE SET TO DEPART THE WOODS IMMEDIATELY. BUT ONE GLANCE INTO THE HOVER WAGON'S REAR VIEW MIRROR WAS ALL THE WARNING THEY RECEIVED...
BARGE SKULLCRACKER WAS RIGHT BEHIND THEM!!!
WHERE'D MOKE RUN SCREAMING OFF TO?
BEATS ME. CARE TO FINISH OFF HIS SODA?
END.

ver so soon!? That's what I'm saying too! Let's pause to bask in the brilliance that is Jay Fos-
tt, folks. Put on your sunscreen first because he is one bright, shiny star! Seriously, the man
st keeps getting better, right? Right!?

nd that is why we are ending the *Little Green Men* graphic novel series.

Pause for dramatic effect)

ut don't worry because there is more *Little Green Men* on the way! How can we be ending
e graphic novels and still have more *Little Green Men* on the way, you ask? What a fantas-
c question. You must be at the top of your class. The answer is- look for the *Little Green Men*
)S Game Application on an iPhone near you! That's right, *Little Green Men* is going to be a
deo game! With super-fun-game-play and a new storyline, *Little Green Men* may yet conquer
e world!

nd what about Jay Fosgitt, you ask? My, my, you are an astute reader. Well, don't you worry
bout Jay! We still have him locked down in the basement drawing Ape Entertainment's next,
reat, all-ages property- **DINO DUCK!** If you are a fan of Jay and the work he's done on *Little
reen Men* (and who here isn't?!) then you are going to love watching Jay cut loose in the cre-
aceous era when monkies and cave-ducks competed for species dominance (hint: the mon-
eys win)!

the first volume, I regaled the readers with the origin story of *Little Green Men*. In the second
olume, I took things to a whole new level and drew a one-page story (written by co-creator
rent Erwin). For this final finale, I decided I would top even those achievements. I thought
ng and hard, debated the merits of a thousand ideas, made detailed plans describing the
ost ambitious, incredible, astounding story ever thought up by Man. This was to be not only
y crowning achievement but a crowning achievement for ***humanity as a whole!***

hen the deadline hit and I had to scramble at the last second and settle for drawing a pin-up.
still hope you enjoy it half as much as I know you enjoyed the rest of the book!
major props to Tim Durning for the outstanding color job).

ook for us on your iPhone real soon and, until then, remember-
ven a small step can be the first of a big adventure!

David Hedgecock
San Diego, CA

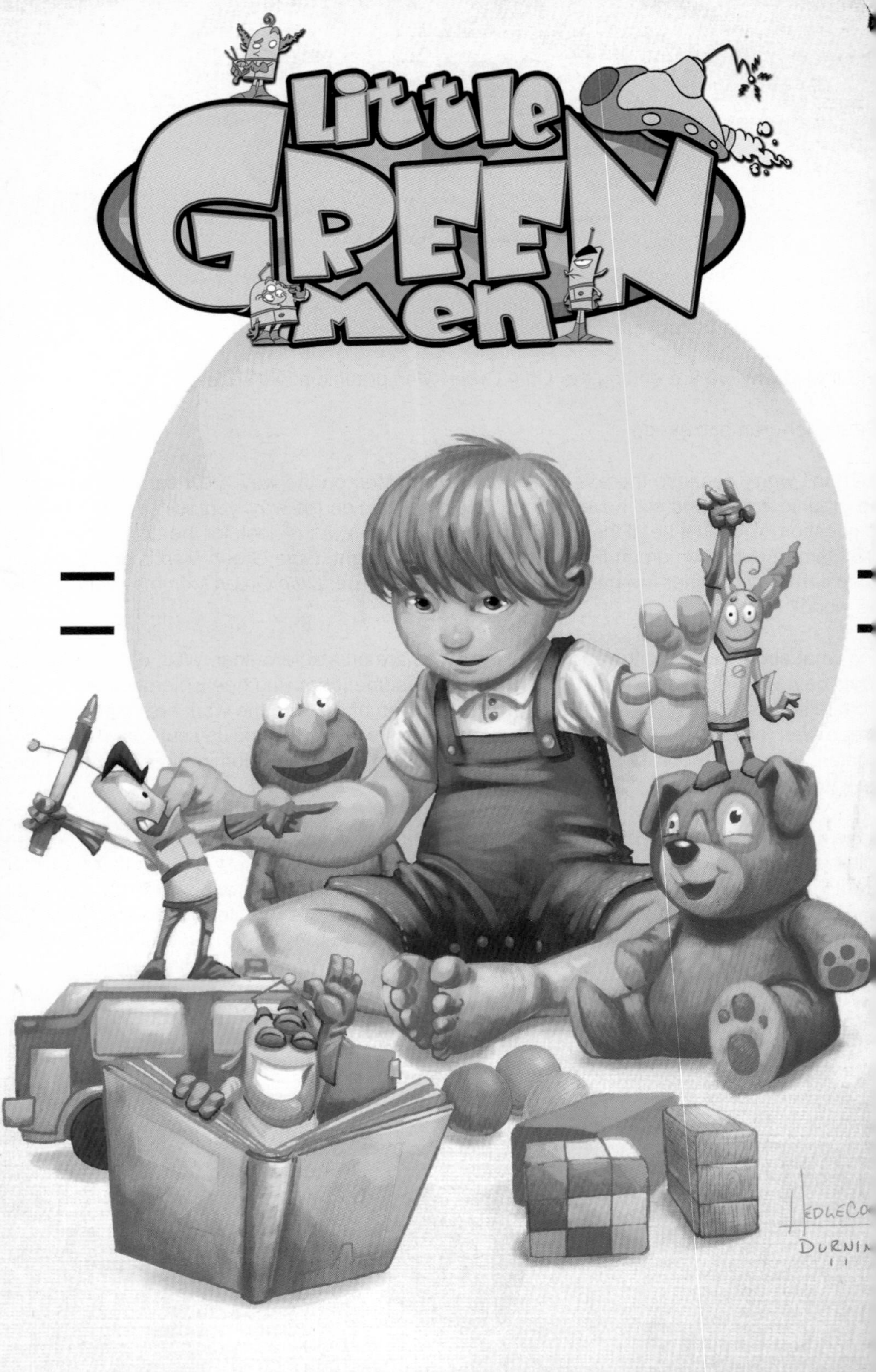
Little GREEN Men

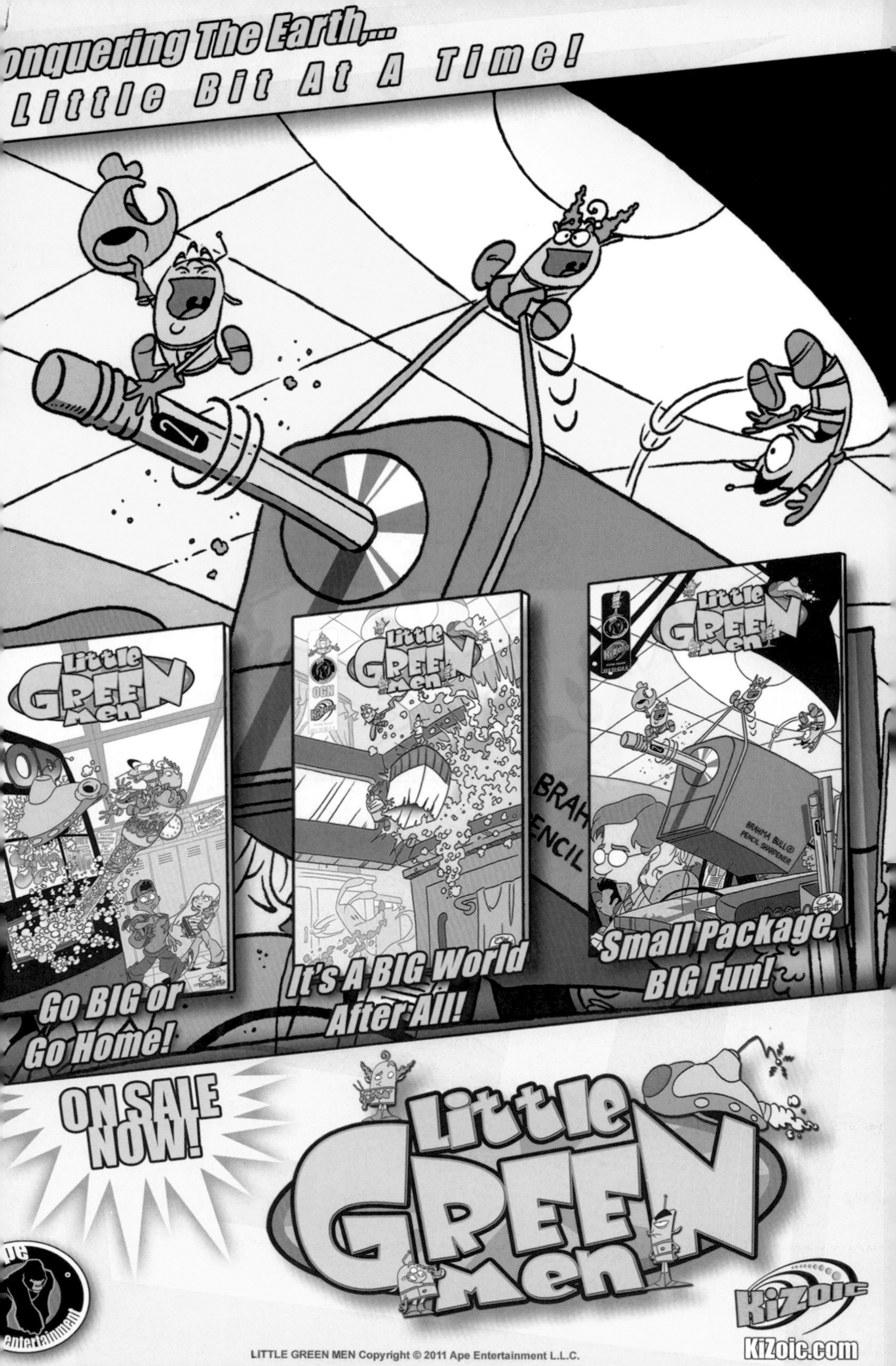
onquering The Earth,...
Little Bit At A Time!
Go BIG or Go Home!
It's A BIG World After All!
Small Package, BIG Fun!
ON SALE NOW!
Little GREEN Men
KiZoic.com

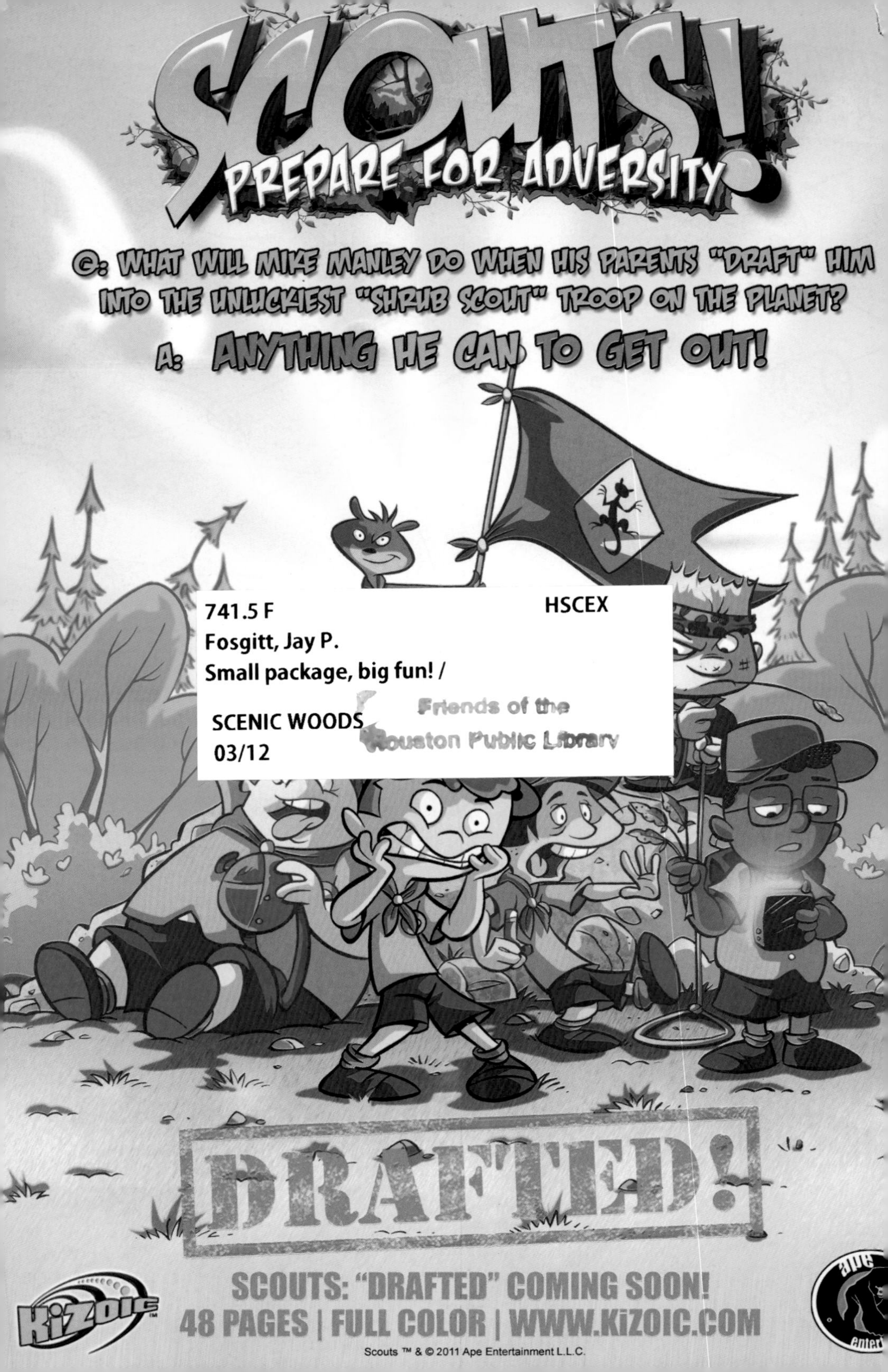
SCOUTS!
PREPARE FOR ADVERSITY
Q: WHAT WILL MIKE MANLEY DO WHEN HIS PARENTS "DRAFT" HIM INTO THE UNLUCKIEST "SHRUB SCOUT" TROOP ON THE PLANET?
A: ANYTHING HE CAN TO GET OUT!
DRAFTED!
SCOUTS: "DRAFTED" COMING SOON!
48 PAGES | FULL COLOR | WWW.KIZOIC.COM
KiZOIC™
Scouts ™ & © 2011 Ape Entertainment L.L.C.